CW00857427

Blood lust

Foreword

Richard Ashcroft is an habitual criminal who forms a doomed relationship with a muslim girl.
Whilst in prison on a previous sentence he encounters a man who killed someone before and conversations with him sets the demons loose in ashcroft.

He has a bloodlust that is not easily satisfied and each time he kills he has a strange ritual of leaving an ancient gold coin behind with the body.

Can the police capture him as he strikes time after time and becomes the most prolific serial killer they have ever encountered.

To Janet a special lady
Enjoy the Read
Dave Ginnelly xx

David Bishop (Art work)
Betty Adams (ProofReader)
Lisa Parker (Typing)

Acknowledgements

Reagan Day (Nuneaton Princess who beat cancer.)
Owen Jones (A Lion amongst bullies.)
Lisa Ashby. Jason Ashby
Andy Crampton (R.I.P)
Rosie Goodwin
Nicki T James. Angie Murphy

All of the above people either supported me financially or encouraged me to continue writing at them moments when I did not feel like doing so.

The prompting and the praise from these people ensured that I picked the pen up once again.

I thank you all sincerely.

About the author

Dave Ginnelly has released three previous books all available in paperback or kindle.

Dave Ginnelly - Author is a facebook page where is it possible to read excerpts of previous books for free.

Wellies and Warders. (best seller)

Never a Dull Moment.

It's a Dog's Life.

Chapter One

Richard Ashcroft had sat on this self same wall on numerous occasions in the past after being released from other sentences, but the one he had just completed was his longest yet.

He had just endured being incarcerated for the best part of two years and six months of a four year sentence for the supply of class A drugs in the shape of cocaine amongst other smaller varieties of drugs.

It had been very much a difficult sentence notwithstanding the amount of time he had served he had also had some problematic cell mates to test his resolve.

More worrying at this moment in time though was the absence of anyone to greet him at the gates, which had never happened before and was causing him great concern to say the least as he reached for his pouch and proceeded to make yet another loosely hand rolled cigarette. Peter Simmons a friend who had been discharged with him on the same day albeit on different charges and sentence had waited with him on the off chance of a lift had also become restless as time passed. "What you going to do Rick" he had asked as he grew impatient. Richard had never been bothered about being called Rick or Ricky and the only abbreviation he had actually detested was Dick and at this moment in time that's exactly what he felt a dick.

It was an uncomfortable embrace when he parted company and waved Pete off and sat back on the wall to make yet another roll up cigarette and gather his thoughts.

His partner Julie had always accepted the lay of the land throughout their turbulent relationship and took the good times with the bad and accepted the harsh reality her partner may end up in prison and away from the family home should he have the misfortune to be arrested during the pursuit of the shady activities.

But Rick, on reflection,had sensed something was a little amiss when a few prison visits had been missed and his incoming mail had become a little bit erratic and when it did actually arrive the length of them had lessened and the words of love and terms of endearment had certainly vanished from the content.

He decided to vacate the area after enduring the odd passing prison officers sneers and sniggering innuendoes because it was all proving to be slightly embarrassing with all of the realisation he had actually been sat outside of the prison for a period of two hours and "fuck that" he thought. I,m a free man and it,s time to celebrate and so with that he blew a fond kiss in the direction of Armley prison in leeds and as always promised himself faithfully that was to be his last spell and he would never darken its doors again.

It was always said with the best of intentions but it would most certainly be down to good fortune should he manage to remain out because he certainly had no intentions of steering clear of what he deemed to be the lucrative profits involved with all he had ever know for many years which was the sale of illicit drugs.

He made his way into the centre of Leeds and then decided that if Julie wasn't in any rush to come and meet him then neither would he be to meet her.

He would deal with the domestic implications later. There would be nothing new there as they had always had a turbulent relationship and he doubted that would ever change now.

He was almost fifty now and had spent perhaps a third of that behind bars and Julie had been loyal and faithful until now and although he was still quite angry he knew in his heart he could forgive her anything and he chose to clear it from his mind her failure to appear outside of the prison to meet him.

Perhaps she was simply busy with their two beautiful sons Kyle and Troy that they had.

Choose whatever problems seemed to be hatching in his life they could never compare to the recent cellmate he had to share with. John Davison, who had no qualms about discussing the fact of how he had strangled the life out of his poor deceased wife and received an eight year sentence for manslaughter for doing so.

Night after night Rick would need to listen in graphic detail about the fateful night when the incident had taken place and even though the man was coming to the back end of his sentence and due for release he spoke as if it had taken place yesterday.

He would recount frenziedly the events that had taken place and glean some sort of morbid satisfaction about the fact she was no longer in existence.

He had listened, intently so often he could repeat word for word what was about to occur next leading up to the demise of the poor lady in question.

He would want to jump off the bed regularly and set about the man and beat him because he certainly did not in any way condone the man's actions and his sympathies definitely lay with the now deceased lady in question.

Although it proved difficult to restrain himself he knew he must do so or it would jeopardize his own early release but in reality he really wanted to smash the man's face to a pulp for the pain and suffering the woman must have certainly gone through.

They would both have places of work within the prison to occupy them throughout the day and therefore it was possible to limit the time spent together but unfortunately on the evening when the cell door was closed for the rest of the night there would be no hiding place from this man's insane ramblings.

Anyone who goes in a prison will readily agree that one of the worst things to contend with is once the door opens with a new arrival. It's the luck of the draw if you get a regular run of the mill criminal as opposed to a rapist or a murderer. You, yourself, have no say what so ever in the matter and Rick had certainly been given the short straw on this occasion.

The evening could begin with reasonable, normal conversation but at some stage of the night the man's obsession with the slaying of his wife would rise to the surface. It was inevitable that he would re-enact every single moment of that fateful night.

Rick had grown accustomed to hearing it and would often pick his newspaper up to read while the other prisoner would pace up and down the cell rambling incoherently to himself in the belief that Rick was still listening.

Lunacy at it's finest Rick would think to himself and the need to get out of there could not come quickly enough.

He thought his release would never come but come it had and he now meandered from one public house to another in search of one of his favourite past times, drugs and in particular cocaine.

He wasn't going to let Julies non-appearance spoil the festivities. He was free and like the proverbial kid in the candy shop he wanted it all and he wanted it NOW!!

He was from Dewsbury a small cotton mill town not far from Leeds. Perhaps eight miles but he felt in no rush to get back there for now especially considering the recent events.

It did not take him too long whilst drinking his pint to observe a little untoward activity by the gentleman's toilets albeit done that swiftly that the regular layman would miss it but to the trained eye of a drug dealer such as himself it shone like the beacon on a lighthouse.

Contact was soon made and once the purchase of a small clip bag of finely powdered cocaine was exchanged he would spend the next ten minutes behind the cubicle door consuming and savouring what he had long since missed and almost immediately his problems no longer existed
Problems!! What problems??

He had tried to contact julie on the home landline but all to no avail so he decided to spend the rest of the day having yet more cocaine and consuming copious amounts of larger and doing what the majority of prisoners do on their first day of freedom.

The rest of the day went by in a blur and early evening soon put in an appearance and he took the decision to catch a train over to his hometown to see if any yellow ribbons had been tied around trees to commemorate his return although he doubted it very much.

The cocaine had stimulated him by now and he feasted his eyes on the few female passengers in close proximity to him on the train. He ogled one after another although none of them made any sort of eye contact with him preferring to ignore him in his drunken state.

Alcohol has a much stronger effect on someone who has been abstinent for any great period of time and Rick would be no different.

Having said that it did not stop him partaking in a few more beverages outside of dewsbury railway station, at a public house, while he emptied the contents of his clip bag he had happily chosen to pay £40 for earlier.

He came across a few old school friends and even one who had been in prison with him a few years previously. He laughed inwardly at how people's paths in life took different twists and turns and how perhaps if given a second chance in life it could maybe be himself who turned out to be a plumber and the man sat across from him reversed roles and   he was the habitual criminal. But it wasn't to be and such is life i'm afraid.

It's fate and we are all dealt a specific hand of cards to play and we either take what's in the pot or we go bust.

There's no second chances. You get one hand at life and it's for you to play and ultimately it's your choice if you make it a success or a failure.

He had already bust a few good poker hands and readily accepted he was never destined for any great success and realised he would spend his life with more of the down side than he ever would living the dream and the good life.

But on the plus side he still had a beautiful partner that loved him and their two children.

Or did he?

He exchanged pleasantries with his present company and after a few hurried arrangements to meet up again soon he made for the door with the realisation he was a little worse for wear now with the amount of alcohol he had consumed.

He chose to walk around for a little attempting to sober up because the last thing he wanted to do right now was have an altercation with Julie when he had only been out of prison for a matter of hours.

He visited a local take away and got himself some supper following the misguided conception that nutrition quickly assists in the sobering up process. It never had before so why this particular occasion was likely to be any different was anyones guess. He was hungry anyway and he doubted very much a plate of food would be sat on the dining table in the family home. God how he hated being an apologist he seemed to be always saying sorry to Julie for one thing or another in almost all of the time they had been a couple.

He jumped into a taxi and made his way to the small detached home they shared by the local cemetery whilst all the time rehearsing his speech and excuses for where he had been all day and also anticipating the lecture he would receive that the children had waited and waited but had gone to bed tired.

He paid the fare and stood outside mustering the courage to walk through the door and noticing the downstairs lights on counted to ten, placed his hand on the handle, and walked in and declared in a joking manner "Hi Honey , I'm home!

To his horror there sat a couple of complete strangers and the rather thick set man jumped to his feet, grabbed Rick by the throat and in no uncertain terms demanded to know what the fuck did he think he was doing just walking into THEIR family home.

Rick was dazed and confused as he found himself in an heap on the small garden at the front of the house.

To say he was shocked would be an

understatement as the man continued to throw verbal threats at rick and mention of putting him in an hospital bed.

He wasn't prepared to give him the slightest opportunity to carry out his threat and he hurdled the fence and scampered down the street.

His head was racing! What on earth had just taken place? He had never been this confused and he ran and ran until he was completely out of breath and exhausted.

He found himself in the local park and rested up by sitting on a bench and took the decision to stay there the night, rest up, and gather his thoughts try as he may though sleep would not come easily.

Chapter Two

Come here girl! Come here! He heard a strange male voice command his dog to come to heel as he opened one of his eyes in a very disorientated state just in time to see them departing albeit with the man looking over his shoulder in disgust.

Rick sat up and began to roll a cigarette. How long had he lain there? What was the time even?

He noticed a few shabbily dressed men shuffling about in one direction or another and suddenly realised that he himself must have appeared to be one of the town's many down and outs who slept either in the bushes or benches of the park.

He had one colossal headache and not just to do with a hangover but more so what had unfolded with the previous night's events.

He was glad he had not got any drugs left because today he would need to stay focused and try to make sense of it all and drugs would only cloud the issue.

He sat there for what seemed an eternity but in reality was the best part of an hour before gathering his thoughts and exiting the park because in all honestly nothing would be resolved by sitting here and he knew that but was very much shell shocked and unable to move for that initial period.

He had many friends who lived on the nearby Dewsbury Moor estate although he doubted they would be out of bed at this ungodly hour. Far too early for them because their lifestyle was a very similar one to his own involving drugs and late nights.

So he ambled about the estate aimlessly for a while but as he rounded the corner on one of the streets he took a step back when he noticed, parked up, his old white bedford van which he used to let a friend borrow to clean wheelie bins as a sideline for himself to account for money accrued from drug deals.

He approached the van with caution but upon looking through the window he could clearly see the jet wash used for the work and also a few bags and odds and ends.

It was parked outside a married couples home he knew. Caron Morton and Mick Fox had been together for many years and although he hadn't seen much of them prior to his recent sentence he still regarded them as close friends but he certainly wasn't about to make the same mistake as the previous evening and just open the door and walk into the abode.

From the very moment he had left the jail everything had been surreal so by reckoning there was a good chance that even Mick and Caron no longer lived here.

His fears were cast aside by the opening of the door and the big familiar smile associated with Mick was plain to see.

Mick threw his arms around Rick in a tight bear hug and that felt good he thought because finally here was someone glad to see him home.

He was greeted like a long lost son and while Caron cooked them both a full English breakfast Mick relayed the little information he knew to Rick although rather guarded in his conversation because he did not want to give him any misinformation considering the troubled manner of his friend.

Julie and a male 'friend' had dropped the van outside of the address and given Caron the keys and notified her that a few personal belongings were also in the back of the van.

After the completion of the meal they both went outside to discover that alongside the jet wash were a few black bin liner full of Rick's clothes and a few strange additions like a bag of knitting needles and wool.

Where would the women of today be without the obligatory bin liners. Rick wouldn't be the first or the last to see his whole life dumped in bags on doorsteps or in this instance a bedford van.

They could both see the hurt on Rick's face and without hesitation offered him a place to rest his head until he got to the bottom of it all.

He gathered his belongings from the van all expect the knitting material as he doubted very much that he would be sitting about for long periods casting off and producing any knitwear.

His life had suddenly become a train crash. He had been left with nothing and it was etched all over his face.

She had obviously ran off with another man and he had certainly never envisaged a situation such as the one he found himself in now.

Obviously he was hurt by her actions but at this moment in time he pined for his children and it was as if his ribs had been removed.

Countless fathers go through this same scenario and then are portrayed as some evil demon when in reality it,s the mother, very quickly as well i might add, starting another family and the pretence of the father being a demon needs to be maintained.

It's wrong on so many levels but it will continue while we have a legal system stacked in favour of the female.

Maybe he had burnt all of his bridges in respect of the relationship but nobody has the god given right to reach the decision of depriving a father any access to his children and Rick felt very aggrieved.

His one consolation was that while he was inside he had lost a little of his remission. The time allocated for good behaviour. So at least he had no parole conditions to adhere to because already he would have been in breach of them conditions and liable to be recalled back to the prison.

The evening's conversation was very limited considering they had not seen each other for a long period of time and because Ricks mind raced as he attempted to come to terms with all of the recent events and after a few uncomfortable silences he took the decision to retreat to his room and sleep in his first comfortable bed since his release.

Sleep would not come easily though through musing over events and the sounds of Mick and Caron's love making in the next room would only add to the restlessness.

He woke quite early the following morning as most prisoners will confirm it is very difficult to achieve a regular sleeping pattern upon release from any institution and to sleep through even until mid morning is virtually impossible.

He made his way down the stairs being careful to make little noise and disturb his hosts and after a quick bowl of cereal he left a note on the dining table thanking them for all their assistance and promised to return later that evening.

He jumped into his van and to his great surprise and relief the engine turned over at it's first attempt and he drove away to find the nearest garage to fill the tank.

"What a lovely morning" the male cashier said as he paid for his purchase and Rick wanted to smash his face straight through the back wall as it was far from this so called lovely morning as far as he was concerned and he vacated the premises as quickly as he could for fear of reacting in an aggressive manner.

He made himself count to ten before he drove away because there was no doubt about it than in his present frame of mind he could quite easily kill someone. He was in a very murderous mood and he had the urge to cause someone, anyone, serious harm and these moods needed to be quelled. If that was possible!

He could not recall ever being this angry and he supposed someone would need to pay although he certainly did not wish it to end with him, yet again, on a prison exercise yard.

He would need to curb his behavior until such a time that should a violent altercation placate his mood then let it be in a controlled situation with no witnesses or police involvement.

He parked the van up by the local train station and proceeded to walk into the town centre and do everyday things like any normal member of the public but he was a walking time bomb waiting to explode.

The year was 2017 and the tory government had made things very difficult to simply register for unemployment at any office throughout the country and Dewsbury would be no different.

Rick soon discovered that nothing at all ran smooth in this office and he was instructed to call some number to complete the formalities. Once reality set in that not one civil servant was available to speak to him his anger grew yet again and rather than get embroiled in all of this government red tape he knew before he even kicked the doors open as he left that he would be returning to a life of crime.

The security guard at the D.H.S.S shouted something about damage to the door and Rick half turned to walk back towards him but in that one momentary glance between both men's eyes the man, very wisely, went back into the building closing the door behind him.

Rick walked away and found himself sat on a bench in the bus station and reflected on how everyone and everything was pissing him off today and now to make matters worse he now had a drunken bum motioning to him every two minutes. He had heard the noise but hadn't even realised it was directed at him in a broad glaswegian accent "See you Jimmy" "giz some money ya bastard"! The insults were coming thicker and faster with the knowledge he was making little or no headway in his pleas for money and before Rick could get up and walk away the drunken tramp was stood in front of him issuing him threats and demanding money and thrusting his hand into Rick's face.

Rick stood up and could make no sense of

half of what the man was saying in his drunken scottish accent.

A passer by demanded he leave Rick alone and in that one moment he was distracted Rick managed to walk away but not without having to listen to countless insults declaring that Rick was "A wimpy basta".

Rick looked back in a blind rage to glare at the man but also to take the opportunity to register every little detail of this grubby little scotch bum.

He had every intention of meeting him again and on the next occasion the outcome would not be so favourable for the man.

But for now his options were limited in how he could pass his day and it was inevitable he ended up in the pub and though it may give him the chance to maybe glean any further information of his partner's where abouts it would ultimately lead to one of his favourite past times which was consuming alcohol and getting drunk.

On this particular day though he got very much drunker than what he would normally do and was even asked to leave a few of the town centre pubs through being a nuisance.

He was no company for no one really and not one person wanted to engage him in conversation to be honest.

After being asked to leave his last pub he did not want to run the risk of drink driving and so jumped into the back of a taxi all the while mumbling away to himself which caused the pakistani driver a little concern and once he declared they had reached the destination he swore at the driver that he "no longer lived at this fucking address".

They had pulled up outside the home of himself and his previous partner. He had returned to the house just as a homing pigeon does to a coop but the taxi driver was none too pleased and demanded his fare but Rick demanded another destination and indicated that he go the car park by the train station.

By now the driver was getting very concerned that his passenger was not going to pay and when Rick caught him looking in the rear view mirror he showed him a wad of notes in his hand but began to realise he did not like the drivers attitude one bit and asked him to put the light on in the back which the driver did not object to doing because it gave him the opportunity to recognize Rick's face, should he need to if anything was amiss at a later date.

Rick would not mind him seeing his face as they pulled into the car park because it would be the last face he would ever see again.

He had loosened the shoelace from his boot and after entwining it around his fingers very tightly he brought it round and over the man's head and very quickly around his throat and strangled the life out him while his body kicked and thrashed until no resistance remained and he was lifeless.

With the light of the interior of the cab being on he now realised what his cell mate had described about the bulging eyes because he was now staring straight into them and it was a very surreal moment with the realisation that he also had an erection which he found to be very strange.

In Rick's frenzied state he had become fully aroused but surely there could be no sexual gratification in killing another person especially when it was male.

He tried to put it to the back of his mind as he rifled through the man's pockets.

He had no qualms about committing another crime by robbing the man as he had already committed the very ultimate crime. Murder! He had done his first kill and the excitement it had created would give no warning of the mayhem that was now to come.

While he emptied the man's pockets he also hit the jackpot by finding almost three thousand pounds and several tiny wraps of heroin which many of the taxi drivers in the North sell as a lucrative sideline. It's a big problem but Rick wasn't bothered because he had completed his first kill and was more financially secure than he could have even imagined at the beginning of the day.

He turned off the lights and left his corpse there all wide eyed and made his way towards his van and still with the lace around his hand, wrapped tight, made his exit from the area.

In his haste what he failed to realise was a little old lady at the edge of the car park had seen him running away.

His only good fortune was that she believed him to be running away from paying his fare rather than what had just taken place.

Mrs Robinson would return at a later date to haunt him and become his worst nightmare.

Chapter Three

Detective inspector James O'Dowd had been through a very illustrious career with many commendations but had now become quite bored with it all and was simply marking time until his imminent retirement.

Nothing caught his attention no more

because everything just seemed so predictable and routine.

"Looks like robbery" said detective sergeant Phil Williams when he reached the scene where the taxi driver was slumped in the front seat by his steering wheel.

Now even though the inspector realised this man must be someone's husband and father the spark just wasn't there no more. Everything just seemed so humdrum and routine as he half-heartedly poked about and rummaged in the footwell of the car searching for any clues. He picked up one of the small heroin wraps that Rick must have dropped and after taking a look inside the wrap he didn't need much confirmation of the contents because he had seen it many times before and now he had even less sympathy with the driver because he now reached the conclusion it was a drug deal that had taken place and gone wrong.

He hated drug dealers with a passion and simply went through the motions while inwardly thinking let them all kill each other in similar settings and it would make his job much easier.

Detective Constable Linda Peterson said "i think there's two of them robbed him Guv! One in the front and one sat behind him"!

There were no flies on Linda he thought. She was quite a clever girl who quickly read any situation and her presumption that there was maybe one in the front doing the deal while the rear passenger done the deed would probably prove to be correct.

They had a strained working relationship and had done for the previous six years because when Linda had joined the C.I.D they both had a brief fling with each other that due to marriage commitments had finally fizzled out albeit quite bitterly at first. At one stage Linda considered asking for a transfer but by doing so would have needed to answer awkward questions and to be honest the affair had been kept very low key and no one was even aware of it so the decision was reached to keep the workplace in a strictly professional manner although recently she had began to feel she had been overlooked on a few occasions when promotions had become available. She could not believe she had slept with him in the first place but she was a junior and he regaled her with stories of the Yorkshire ripper Peter Sutcliffe when he was first arrested and detained at Dewsbury.

She didn't know how much of it was fact or fiction but she was a little in awe of him. Perhaps a little too much and as he aged she saw the boredom etched on his face and she also couldn't wait until he retired.

She did a lot more investigating nowadays than he ever could and she couldn't wait until the day he was given his retirement carriage clock and then maybe she could get the promotion she felt she rightly deserved.

"He don't listen to none us no more Linda" said constable John Phelps "You're wasting your breath"!

John had always fancied Linda but never had the courage to tell her because he never once imagined she would give him the time of day. He was also married but in any police force countless officers will tell you the hours worked put a terrible strain on most marriages and the inevitable affairs take place.

Their eyes would often meet during their shift but on this particular day it was not exactly the ideal setting finding a body between that stare as they both poked their heads into the interior of the car. They were both criminal detectives in the main but should any murder take place these would be the four responsible to investigate matters.

Inspector O'Dowd made his way from the scene, lighting his pipe, and declared he was satisfied it was a robbery gone wrong and nothing else seemed to contradict that conclusion so it was a case of back to the station and go through all of the formalities of completing the paperwork, informing the press and putting an appeal out for witnesses. Nothing else could be done at this moment in time.

Chapter Four

Rick woke up in a very addled state and tried not to believe what he had done last night had ever taken place. He wanted it to be a bad dream! A nightmare but alas once he started to get dressed and he felt the large wad of notes he knew it had happened. The thing that concerned him most was he did not express or feel the slightest remorse. In fact he was in a state of excitement as he realised he, once again, had an erection.

He quickly sat back on the bed when the door knocked and Caron came in with a tray of breakfast and a cup of tea and asked him if he was ok as they hadn't heard him come in the night before. He assured her everything was fine and apologized for being a little anti social lately but he was just trying to come to terms with all his recent misfortune and he would be fine in a week or so but right now he preferred to be a tortoise with his head inside the shell.

They were both fine with him being there and told him to have the run of the house and come and go as he pleased.

He enjoyed watching how good and strong their relationship was and he recalled his own relationship being of a similar nature but it was no good dwelling or that would just make him sad and in the wrong frame of mind.

He was rather happy instead because of the previous night's events and even though he knew that he should feel different, because he had taken someone's life he couldn't bring himself to do so. Instead he wanted to hear every single snippet of news and relive that moment over and over again.

He wasn't to know but before very long the memory would fade and the urge would return because he had dipped his toes in the water re-living something is all well and good but re-enactment would be his only solution. Doing the deed and in those moments no one would be safe because this wasn't about specific targets. This was to be victims chosen at random and on the spur of the moment. He showered and changed clothes and made his way downstairs and placed one hundred pound on the table and Mick said "Don't be silly! We don't want all that"! But Rick insisted and told them to treat each other and go out for a meal or something.

Once they had left the house he quickly surfed

all the local tv channels and teletext and was pleased to hear it had been described as a robbery and although he noticed the appeal for witnesses he was quite sure he escaped any needless attention whilst making his escape. He felt comfortable for the time being with the large amount of notes in his pocket but he knew it wouldn't last forever and he had no intentions on setting foot in the D.H.S.S again 'fuck government handouts' he thought. The place is like a minefield now and nobody knows if they are likely to get any money from one day to the next.

He suddenly remembered that a few years before he had burgled a museum in Leeds and stolen about eleven ancient gold coins that had originated from the Inca period in Mexico and obviously he had great difficulty getting rid of them because even on the black market these items were very difficult to dispose of and so he had secreted them under the garden shed at his previous home until such a time as he hopefully found a reputable and reliable dealer.

His plan for today would be to retrieve them at the earliest opportunity in case the new residents of his home decided to replace the present shed at any time.

He, firstly, checked all of the bin liner bags in the back of the van on the off chance Julie had put the bag of coins into one of them because she had been aware he had hidden them under the shed and he also had to hope she hadn't taken them with her to start her new life although he doubted this very much as she wouldn't have a clue what to do with them. He searched the back of the van thoroughly and once again laughed at the knitting needles and wool and reminded himself that due to this affair the last thing she had been doing while he was inside was a bit of knitting.

He drove around the estate for a little while and past his old home to confirm that the shed was in the exact same spot it had always been. It had always been his favorite hidey-hole. His little man cave where he would just weigh out his drugs but also retire to there for a little privacy at times. A modern day retreat which more and more men seem to retire to.

He would need to choose a more quiet moment to return to retrieve his ill gotten gains so he whiled away the hours buying a few new clothes and visiting shops previously unknown to him due to his spell in prison. Lots of new fashions shops on the high street and he quickly spent a few hundred pound filling different bags with all the latest brand names.

He became hungry and visited a small cafe on one of the back streets because he preferred the smaller ones as he believed a lot more attention was accorded to the paying customer.

No other customers were in the cafe as he

struck up a conversation with the bleached
blonde girl behind the counter although the
time had long since been and gone when the
colouring needed doing again because all the
roots were showing through.

He looked her up and down from behind as she
prepared his meal and discussed menial
matters like the weather amongst other boring
subjects. He decided she would have had a few
failed relationships and was now single and
working here to make ends meet.

She had quite a reasonable figure and had
kept herself in good shape and he found
himself aroused looking at her which
surprised him because this was the first time
he had even thought of engaging in sexual
activities since his release from prison.
After he had completed his meal he patted the
chair and motioned for her to sit with him
which she did willingly.

It was possible the first sort of male
attention she had encountered for a good while
and she was certainly making the most of it.
The signs were easy to pick up by Rick that
she was lusting for him too and especially
when she asked him to just watch the shop while
she went to use the wash room and came out with
significantly more makeup on than when she
went in.

She was spinning her web and was hoping to
get Rick caught up in the netting. She had
obviously done this before and probably on a

lot more occasions than she would care to admit.

Her name turned out to be Paula and it had reached the stage were no conversation was needed and Rick knew he would never receive a slap across the face so as Paula cleared the table he simply slipped his hand up her skirt and stroked her inner thigh at the top and brushed against her tiny panties. Paula gasped and said "you're a quick worker" but there was no resistance as Paula opened her legs wider for Rick to place even more fingers inside her. If it had happened before, as Rick thought, then it had been a while because her juices were flowing out like a waterfall and the only thing that stopped proceedings was the noise of the bell that indicated someone had entered the cafe.

The stranger who entered wishing to have a tea and scone would never have been able to even begin to imagine what had just taken place as the waitress prepared his tea in a very weak kneed state.

She implored Rick to stay until the stranger had left but he had things to do and promised her he would call on another day. She smiled half heartedly and waved him off but cursed her job believing that would be the last time she would ever see him.

In an ironic way perhaps that would of been a more preferable outcome for her but she was not to know what lay ahead.

Rick had a few beers in the closest pub to his old home and once it got a little dark he made his way through the hedge of the house next door and found himself at the top end of what used to be his own garden and began to urinate against the shed.

For some strange reason anyone who is out stealing will tell you the same story of a need to be using the toilet in one way or another. Who knows if it's an adrenalin thing or what but it's quite a regular occurrence.

After completion of the urinating he lay down flat on the lawn and placed his hand on the bag after a little rummaging about but just as a big hand pulled him to his feet by the scruff of his neck and proceeded to shine a torch in his face.

"You again! You little bastard" he roared as the first punch made contact, he attempted to explain that he had lived there previously but the opportunity never came about as another punch landed square on his jaw and he was dragged along the garden and thrown into the street after another flurry of punches with a firm warning that should he ever be caught within one hundred yards of this home again he would find himself buried under the garden shed.

He had no reason to doubt his threats as he scurried away but the beating was worth it as he untied the string on the little purse to reveal the objects of his desire the gold coins in exactly the same resting place as he had left them.

His jaw felt very tender and that bloke was some size and he was more than happy to take his advise to stay within one hundred yards of his home. In fact he was happy to increase that to one hundred miles. He never wanted to lay eyes on him again. He could keep his home and also his shed he thought as he caressed his jaw and face.

He now not only had a pocket full of money but he also had something in the reserve tank by way of the gold coins. Their historic value meant nothing to him and if all else failed and he needed to he would melt then down considering the recent prices of anything with the gold content in. He would make less of course but this is how he would need to live now he had resorted back to a criminal lifestyle.

The strange thing about it all was this was the very first time he had said it and actually meant it that he intended reforming and staying out but in the space of forty eight hours he had not only re-offended again but he had actually murdered someone.

Even stranger was the fact that he felt no emotion or remorse about any of it and had just took it in his stride as if he had done no more than swatted a fly.

He had become numb to his actions and had he known what lay ahead perhaps it would have

been best to seek professional help.
He had been a sleeping volcano but in the coming period of time he would erupt uncontrollably.

Chapter Five

James O'Dowd arrived at his desk bright and early as he usually did to discover a memo that the chief superintendent wished to see him at the earliest opportunity. He somehow or another knew it wouldn't be for a pat on the back or to receive any praise so he had a quick drink of the whisky in his filing cabinet and braced himself for what was to come.
He had guessed right as the super launched into a tirade about racial tensions in the area due to the murder of the taxi driver and wished to know what headway he had made in finding the persons responsible.
He tried to get a word in but it was

impossible. He had long since learnt to go with the flow of things and come to terms with the pecking order and if the super was going to get a reprimand then that would soon be passed down to the next man in the chain of command which in this instance was himself. The people above no longer seemed to represent the best interests of the men below them and chose to ignore the fact that due to manning levels and limited resources things no longer ran as smoothly as they once did but even so this driver had only been killed a matter of days before.

Dewsbury had long been a hotbed of Islamist extremists with many more incidents than other areas. The youngest suicide bomber had hailed from the area and it was fighting a losing battle nowadays it seemed to change public opinion and the area had changed for the worse many years before he thought and it was also one of the main reasons he could not wait for his retirement.

He wanted to tell his boss that in his opinion it was a drug deal that had turned nasty but it would be folly to do so because any of this information would simply fall on deaf ears because no one would want to listen and he knew before he asked not to even reveal this sort of information to the press because the local community would seize on that and say that the police had planted it.

No one would be prepared to believe the driver

was a drug dealer so that information could never at any time be released into the public domain and as a policeman and a good one at that he felt nowadays his hands were completely tied in the job he no longer felt he could do.

The racist card would be pulled on the police at every opportunity and the one thing James O'Dowd wasn't was a racist. He never had been and never would be.

He never got much chance to say much of anything to his boss and before he knew it he was being ushered out of office with a friendly arm around him reiterating what a sensitive situation "WE had found ourselves in" when in reality the higher up the chain you went the less police work these people did.

Their job seemed to consist of answering the phone to leading notaries within the community and after listening to complaints passing them concerns to others and he now resented the fact that he had to do the same to his colleagues.

What the fuck did they think he could do with the resources he had available.

Had it been a white taxi driver the conversation which had just taken place between them would not have even taken place.

Now that's what he considered to be racism although he would not dare voice his opinion. Instead he made his way back to his office and after having yet another double whisky out of his ever decreasing bottle in the cabinet he called his already overworked colleagues in to instruct them to overlook any other crimes they were investigating and to focus all of their energy on the murder of the taxi driver and to monitor all of the CCTV from the surrounding areas and that they would be required to work late for the foreseeable future which did not go down to well with them. He would also be working late with them but in an ideal world everyone would be able to move along the bus and forget all about someone who had actually traded in death himself through his sale of heroin.

He tried to convince himself of the need to act professionally but his mind set would come back to the same conclusion that the man was scum and the world and especially Dewsbury was a better place without him.

But from a policeman's point of view he also had a killer/killers to find as he sat and studied a few papers and files to do with the case.

He needed 'The Super' off his back so the clock was now ticking for whoever committed the act. The hunt was on!

Chapter Six

Rick had slept soundly for the first time in a long time but that was understandable because for the first time in as long as he could remember he had inhaled some heroin before he went to sleep the evening before.

He had saved the silver paper from a bar of kitkat chocolate bar and 'chased the dragon' up and down a few times and inhaled the smoke from the substance through a tube. He had forgotten how sweet the taste was and how relaxing it could be as he had fallen into a heap on the bed and slept like a baby in a dream like state.

He had taken it before on a few occasions and readily knew the importance of not taking it too often because of it's habit forming nature. He had always taken drugs throughout his life but had always been careful regarding becoming addicted to anything but he still had all of the wraps he had taken from the taxi driver and he saw no harm in having a little taste of the wares which turned out to be of a good quality considering the deep sleep he had just had.

He took a long shower and then changed his clothes for the first time since his release and put on some of his recent purchases and felt very fresh and smart and ready to face the world.

He exchanged a few pleasantries with Mick and Caron whilst they all ate breakfast and he never once now let the name of his ex partner pass his lips because to do so would create a hostile atmosphere and at this moment in time he felt a little more relaxed and able to take the situation in his stride.

After waving them both off under the pretence of attempting to find a job he set off on foot to go about his business which was to try and sell at least one gold coin individually even if he wasn't likely to get the full monetary value.

He left the others on top of the wardrobe in the jeans he had just taken off and kept rolling the one coin between his fingers whilst admiring the appearance of the coin considering how old it must be. It certainly was a thing of beauty but the only thing that mattered to him was any profit margin he may make on the sale of it.

He called to see a few friends he hadn't seen for a while but everyone of them was of the same opinion that it would be a very awkward item to sell on. He was careful not to mention that he had many more of the same coins because he felt it served no purpose unless a 'fence' could be found who was prepared to buy more.

In the criminal underground it is usually possible to sell just about any item on albeit with the rewards and percentage decreasing at every turn while everyone makes a little profit from the proceeds but for anyone to reap any rewards from these particular items it would need to be a specialist buyer, a collector, who was prepared to show them off now and again but never let them surface in the public domain which would most certainly bring about unwarranted attention.

After a few fruitless telephone conversations it soon became apparent that it would prove difficult to complete any deal at this time.

Rick wasn't exactly without money right now and he hadn't seen his friend Mick Bailey for a good while so he told Mick to forget about making any more business calls and instead ring and arrange for some cocaine to be dropped off instead and that he, Rick, would foot the bill.

He had forgotten how funny Mick could be as they both sniffed the powder and laughed the morning away recounting funny adventures they had both had in the past more often than not to do with prison or the local constabulary.

The rest of the morning was filled with raucous laughter and Rick was much more visibly relaxed but by mid afternoon he decided to go on his way. He had just spent the past few years stuck indoors in a prison cell so he now needed to be outdoors at every opportunity.

He marched along the street with a spring in his step due to the copious amount of cocaine that he had just consumed and heightened euphoria he was now experiencing and all his problems mattered little to him as he strutted like a peacock into the very first public house he came across.

Rick was well known in the area and although most couldn't be described as very close friends there wasn't many pubs he could visit without someone knowing him or knowing of him and he could always find people to engage in conversation and while away the hours.

One of them surprised him by saying he thought Rick lived in Bradford now which was about six miles away, because whilst driving through the area he had seen Kyle and Troy coming out of one of the local catholic schools.

He didn't regard this man as a close friend

who he wished to discuss all of his matrimonial and domestic situation with but after making a mental note of the name of the school and later writing it on a beer mat he promised himself that at some stage the following day he would pay the school a visit out of curiousity to see if it was indeed his children's new place of schooling.

He hoped against hope that it was his children but he knew the man to be a drunkard and perhaps he had mistakenly thought it was the boys. It intrigued him for the the rest of the day and he made himself a point of remembering to set his alarm the moment he got back home.

He decided to have no further alcohol for the remainder of the day therefore ensuring his head would be much clearer the day after.

He ambled into the bus station with the intention of buying the edition of the local newspaper to see what, if any, developments were taking place regarding the recently departed taxi driver.

In the very same area as previously sat the drunkard scotchman with two of his friends passing a bottle from one to the other. Their eyes met briefly with each other and the drunk had either not remembered the confrontation or due to Rick's piercing stare it had made him much more sheepish as he broke eye contact and stared to the floor.

The matter would not be forgotten easily as

far as Rick was concerned and it was if the man had a big neon arrow above him pointing down as if to say KILL ME !!

His card was certainly marked and had been firmly set as the next target in the diary to meet his maker. He would need to stalk the man at another time and choose him moment carefully to cajole him away from the busy town centre but for now he moved away from the area rather uncomfortably realizing he, yet again, had an almighty erection.

This disturbed him more than anything due to the fact that it was a male victim again and where was any sexual gratification coming from in that.

It was a strange sensation and one he would prefer not to have in all honestly.

He wandered around the town and before he knew it found himself outside of the cafe where Paula worked and he had been walking past until she had knocked the window, excitedly and encouraged him to come inside.

The brief encounter they had previously had would want Paula to reverse the sign to say CLOSED and physically dive on Rick but as in most instances regarding women she would wish to take things slowly and enjoy the chase.

She sat across from him at the table and they both discussed various matters while they discovered more about each others backgrounds and he cared little about telling her he had recently left prison because he imagined that he wasn't the first rough diamond bad boy that she would have experienced considering the boring life she led she would welcome the excitement and attention that she was receiving.

They brushed legs against each other awkwardly under the table and the only thing that stopped matters proceeding further was the arrival and departure of numerous customers and she cursed the fact that she hadn't bolted the door when Rick first entered because he was now leaving ,yet again, after paying for his coffee and she doubted she would see him again.

He promised he would come and meet her once she closed the cafe at 6pm and take her for a few drinks but many had said it before him and she doubted the promise would be fulfilled.

Upon leaving Rick went to his pocket to get his gold coin to perform his customary habit of spinning the coin through his fingers but to his shock and horror he realised that in the confusion he may have paid for his coffee with it and made his way back in through the door and after explaining to her it was of sentimental value he insisted she check the contents of the till over and over but she again confirmed that it was not in the till and he must have mislaid it somewhere else.

He knew different though, he had been toying around with it right up to the time of entry to the cafe and it was there somewhere. She apologised about his loss and went about her duties while all the time her hand caressed the coin in her apron pocket. She thought that she could surprise him in a few days and maybe that would ensure further contact with each other if she informed him that she had suddenly found the coin. Or, if as she suspected he did not keep the date or even any further contact, she would be able to treat herself.

He left once again infuriated that he had felt she had lied to him because he didn't have her marked down as the devious sort. He gave her the benefit of the doubt that she had maybe dropped it or overlooked it and if push came to shove he could burgle the premises later or maybe even steal the keys to the cafe later from her handbag.

She looked surprised when he met her as planned at the end of her shift , he had been home to get his van and at first she didn't recognise that it was him .

"Well are you getting in or not" Rick asked and she clambered in rather hurriedly and began to kiss him straight away and desperate for sexual activity but Rick slowed her down and asked her to wait while he found somewhere a little more quiet and private.

He drove to a secluded spot by one of the local cemeteries and they both got into the back of the van and she almost broke the zip to his jeans in her frenzied excitement to release Rick's penis to place her mouth around and then try as she may he did not become aroused and she laughed, teased and taunted him about his lack of prowess and Rick began to feel embarrassed as she teased him mercilessly and he could listen no more as he reached for one of the knitting needles close by and in an instant plunged one deep into her neck and before she could recover from the initial shock he thrust another one into her throat. Now he had an erection although she would never get a chance to see it as the life drained out of her and blood spurted in two different directions and her limp body slumped to the floor of the van.

Rick threw her body to one side and checked the contents of her bag for the keys to the cafe but he needn't have bothered because there plain to see in her purse was the gold coin.

"You fucking lying bitch" he thought to himself. "You had it all along" !

He drained whatever surplus blood he could from her and switched the jet wash on to power clean the inside of the van and both of their bodies and then wrapped hers in an offcut of carpet and got himself prepared ready to dispose of her body.

Although she was now dead he waved his erection in front of her face to tease her "Is this what you wanted bitch?" but she certainly wasn't laughing now.

He was about to masturbate but he would need to turn away from the body fearful that he would leave any DNA evidence.

He ejaculated time after time up the side of the van and sat down for perhaps five minutes totally exhausted by the experience.

He cursed her for lying and trying to steal from him and thought if she wanted the coin that bad he would give it to her so he placed the coin in the palm of her hand and closed her hand into a fist and drove further away from the scene and dumped her , the carpet and the coin a few miles away by the local refuse tip.

He then went home and smoked a little more heroin and went to sleep without a care in the world. He had killed for a second time and not even lost a moment's sleep over it!!!

He had also taken a ring from her finger to replace the coin she so readily craved. It was his own personal trophy to remind him of this evening's fateful events.

Chapter Seven

"Are you fucking joking with me?" bellowed Inspector O'Dowd.

A second body had been found in a matter of days which caused him great concern as he paced up and down whilst demanding a car give him a lift to the scene where a female corpse had been found by a man out walking his dog.

He brushed aside the uniformed constables who were guarding the site without showing any identification at all. They knew not to push the matter there was a time and a place to forget protocol and this was one of them as they looked into the incensed face of their superior.

He made his way down to the area where a forensics team were detailing every inch and item of the murder scene.

"Don't think it's happened here Gov !" one of them remarked and they also informed him that the body seemed to have been chemically cleansed for some strange reason and presented him with a small forensic bag with the coin they had discovered in her hand presuming she may have snatched it from some chain around the murderer's neck or wrist.

It seemed to represent a strong clue but they misguidedly believed it to be what the victim had grabbed to present them with it.

At this time they had no reason to think of any other reasons.

O'Dowd would prefer all of his team to focus on this rather brutal murder as opposed to the first one and fuck racial tensions in this area.

Here was a youngish girl who perhaps had done no wrong her whole life apart from take some wrong twists and turns as in the journey that was life.

Without doubt this was now her worst choice in those twists and turns as he looked at the gaping wounds to her neck and throat.

"Bastard" he thought and this killer was the one he wanted to place in handcuffs at the earliest possible moment.

Someone would have the unenviable task of notifying the next of kin of the girls demise. He had done it a few time earlier in his career and it was never a task he relished doing.

Thankfully he had now reached a stage in his career when someone junior to himself would need to relay the unfortunate news.

The press had gathered like the vultures they are. Always circling and looking to pick at the bones of everyone and everything and they never liked to deal with O'Dowd because he would always have a prepared statement and give out the minimum snippets of information.

In this instance he felt no need to reveal the discovery of the coin because for now that was a part of the police investigation in the exact same manner it serving no purpose to mention the heroin discovered in the taxi drivers car.

He called it withheld information and police business although if he ever felt a need to involve a wider audience he would be the first to line any numbers of journalists up BUT only if it proved beneficial to himself.

He called his team together back at the station and although there was already a board with numerous photos on regarding the first murder he wanted another one set-up immediately with all aspects of the young girl's case and to channel all resources into this but should the superintendent ask to inform him work is being carried out on both cases.

The brutality of the attack on the girl had caused him great alarm and he poured himself a much larger glass of whisky than he normally would and finished it off in one swallow.

He would be the first to admit he had become bored with his job but after the circumstances surrounding the past few days he would readily welcome that boredom returning.

Two murders in two days was certainly not what he wanting presenting with on his arrival at his desk. Firstly he wanted to try and

identify who had been using the cafe recently
but he had already been told that it had no
cameras due to being a very small business and
due to it's backstreet location there was also
a lack of C.C.T.V.

Only the large town centre shops seemed to
be monitored on a regular basis and it's plain
to see that many of the small businesses are
unable to afford the additional security and
as always money talks and also buys added
safety. "Money makes the world go round and
human life is secondary" O'Dowd thought to
himself.

He demanded that all of her past or present
boyfriends be brought in for questioning,
with an arm around their shoulders, but only
under the pretext of helping the police with
their enquiries. No reason to cause any alarm
just yet.

Maybe, just maybe, this murder could be
solved in next to no time and from an
optimistic point of view the case could be
closed sooner rather than later.

In a very large percentage of murders any
police force will tell you that the victim
will have been slain by someone that he or she
knew and he was hoping this would be no
different than any other similar cases
previously investigated.

It was soon confirmed that no sexual activity
had taken place and all of the contents of the

female's handbag were still in place so robbery could also be ruled out.

A past lover jealous of a recent lover or vice versa seemed to be the only options available and although he preferred to keep an open mind he was satisfied that this was the work of a male due to the ferocity of the attack.

Even after death it seemed to appear the perpetrator was intent on meting out further stab wounds to the area with the thin sharp instrument which the pathologist had yet to identify.

Whoever this killer was he was certainly a danger out on the streets and the quicker he was in custody and walking around an exercise yard the better for all concerned.

He ordered everyone to also study the recent release of any violent offenders and check on their whereabouts at the time now he had an established time of death. Things were moving quickly as they always did in a murder investigation but the majority of it was simply akin to building a jigsaw and the need to at first discover the corner pieces and then all of the outline until finally solving the puzzle by locating them odd few pieces.

A lot of the early information is trivial but needs gathering to form the full picture. A building site can go nowhere until the foundations are laid and the same basis applies here. The case cannot go forward until all of the basic groundwork is completed.

In all of O'Dowd's time on the force he had only ever been involved in one cold case, an unsolved murder and he would take the papers and file from the case home with him often for bedtime reading in the hope of spotting something he had overlooked.

He still hoped the case would be solved before he retired because to him it felt like a blemish on his record and gave him a feeling of failure. It could still possibly happen because many cold cases long since shelved had been brought to conclusion in the present era due to the rapid advancement in DNA analysis But one job at a time he thought as he studied what information was at hand regarding the present case.

He had been given a double headache with the two murders quickly in succession.

He thought he was dealing with two different cases and killers and was not to know they were done by the same hand. Had he known this he could very quickly have presumed the likelihood of the person doing the killings would give him a strong indication of the possibility of even further deaths.

But it wouldn't be too much longer before the knowledge smacked him straight in the face with the realisation he had a serial killer on the loose but for now it was simply routine and a case of going through the motions.

No cause for alarm!! Yet!!

Chapter Eight

Rick woke early the next morning and followed his usual routine of showering and shaving to make himself look a little presentable with the intention of going to speak to his children at the school he had wrote the address of on the beermat until he realised that it was in fact a Saturday and that would need to be put on hold.

 He counted up his money and still had a very substantial amount and he gathered up the remaining ten coins and placed them in another pocket and promised himself he would need to be much more careful with them considering what had happened with the one the day before.

He would purchase a kinder surprise chocolate egg from the shop later and use the plastic casing of the toy to conceal his coins in along with the girls ring and insert that up his rectum for safe keeping and away from prying eyes.

All of the morning news while they sat eating breakfast was to do with the discovery of the girl's body and he kept one eye on the TV although never at any time gave the impression that he was overly interested in the events.

It was the first time they had all sat together in the few previous days and Caron remarked about the bruising to Ricks face and he simply told a few half truths.

He admitted that he had visited his previous address to question the occupants about the whereabouts of his previous partner and children and that the man had took offence and set about him. It wasn't far removed from the truth and they both sympathised with him and Caron suggested I go for a few beers with Mick and avoided any trouble spots that may land him back in the prison.

It seemed a good idea because he hadn't spent that much time with them since he had moved in and so they both placed a few football bets on and made for the local working men's club for an afternoon of sport.

Apparently Caron saw Saturdays as an empty

home and the opportunity to catch up on all of the chores that had built up throughout the week. Rick had forgotten what it was like to just relax and unwind and just socialise with normal people and spent the afternoon playing cards and dominoes and watched the football results unfold of which neither of them had any good fortune but needless to say it had been a very pleasurable afternoon but that was all about to change once they got back home and he could tell by the stern look on Caron,s face that something was amiss while she was in a huddled conversation in the dining room with Mick.

"We need to have a word Rick" said Mick and it soon transpired that whilst Caron was doing her chores of stripping beds and gathering clothes to be washed she had discovered lots of wraps of heroin and also the tinfoil Rick had been using to smoke it and he attempted to inform them that it was only on the two occasions he had used it and only to get some respite and bring about sleep but they were seriously offended and not prepared to believe him.

"Why the need for all of them wraps then?" Caron demanded to know, thinking if he had bought them he intended to use it time after time. He couldn't really explain it away by saying that he had actually killed a taxi driver and the wraps were in his pocket now could he?

Without further ado they informed him they wanted him out of their home by the end of the weekend and he should start looking immediately for somewhere to stay.

The atmosphere was very strained and tense and they let him know in no uncertain terms how disappointed they were with him and how disgusted they felt that he had abused their home.

He was angry at himself for being so careless as to leave the drugs lying around and he certainly understood their anger towards him and he apologised as much as he could before he went out the front door in search of somewhere else to reside. He drifted about aimlessly for a while unsure as to what to do and then he suddenly became engulfed with guilt for everything that had taken place the previous week and before he knew it he was stood in front of the prominent building which is St Paulinus Roman Catholic Church right in the middle of the estate and he chose to walk in and light a candle for the two victims. He settled on a pew before kneeling and beginning to pray. Looking around the church seemed to be quite busy but then Rick realised it was a Saturday tea-time and it was time for the confessional box for all Catholics.

Hadn't he , himself, been sent as a small boy to confess his sins and he was unsure as to what to do and what to say. He had always said he had been lying or swearing as a young boy, for his sins, and after saying his penance by praying would quickly run to join his friends and resume the game of football.

He wasn't even sure if swearing or lying was even a sin but he would always be told to confess so he thought anything would do. But on this occasion he had committed the ultimate sin TWICE and as he waited patiently in the queue he turned it over in his head exactly how he would approach this situation and before he knew it he was behind the door and curtain and uttering the words he had memorised as a child.

"Bless me Father for I have sinned, it has been so many years since my last confession" and the priest tells you to proceed.

Rick could not go that extra mile and instead told the priest he only THOUGHT he MIGHT have killed someone and the priest rather alarmed asked him to tell him more but Rick had already exited the confessional box and was knelt praying.

He only looked up, startled, when Father Hinchcliffe had placed his hand on his shoulder and inquired if he could be of any help but by now Rick had rose to his feet and quickly sprinted from the church.

Father Hinchcliffe did not know what to make of the incident and he gave it little thought except to try and place a name to the familiar face that had just sat in front of him but who he had not seen for many years now.

He remembered most children and it was only a matter of time before a name came to his memory banks also.

Rick almost sprinted out of the church in his haste to get away and he cursed himself for opening up to the priest although he knew he hadn't revealed too much and he hoped the priest wouldn't regard the confession as being truthful.

Father Hinchcliffe stood at the entrance, stroking his chin, to his church and attempted to make sense of what he had just heard whilst all the time his eyes followed the confessor right up to the point he vanished around the corner of the street and then he returned into the church and doused all of the candles, prepared the altar for the following morning mass and locked and secured the church for the evening.

That was the first time Rick had been in the church for many years and even though it had remained one of the better maintained buildings in the area it in no way matched the splendor of one of the local mosques in close proximity to it. In fact it looked rather shabby in comparison.

Multiculturalism and in particular the ones of Muslim origin had completely taken the area over.

Rick was not a racist but it saddened him how the neighbourhood and outlying estates seemed to have completely become swamped with immigrants now and there was no turning back. It was out of control but nobody seemed to be able to do much about it.

It had spiralled out of control and the clock could never be turned back now and although he got on with most immigrants he came into contact with the thought would always remain in his mind about the disproportionate level of extremism in this area and the lack of effort to converse and integrate by many of the immigrants in the area.

It was as if some of them had drawn up battle lines many years before and now were not prepared to live in harmony but having said that it didn't apply to all of them and he would soon need to approach a few of them in respect of finding alternative accommodation because it was they who rented out many of the properties within the town.

He walked through a particularly predominant muslim neighborhood with signs in the window indicating rooms or bedsits to rent in a shared capacity .

He viewed a few before making his decision because he needed to take into account the need for privacy considering his recent murderous activities and finally plumped for one that was an upper room that was a little secluded from a few of the other residents who he had no wish to meet. He and the landlord, a practising Muslim. both knew the property was a slum and not fit for human habitation and should the premises be reported to the department of the environment it would be regarded as condemned forthwith.

After an agreement was reached ,that it was possible to move in on the following Tuesday, a form of 'contract' was drawn up and signed. All that remained was Rick to fill the grubby hand that reached out with a total of two months rent. One of which was to cover the month in hand which was customary to cover any damages that may be incurred whilst he lived in the abode.

The landlords eyes lit up when he seen the large bundle of money in his tenants hand and he felt comfortable knowing he would, for once, not be needing to deal with a tenant involved in any number of ongoing sanctions from government benefit offices which seemed to be the case all of the time now. It had given many landlords continuous headaches but this arrangement with Rick seemed perfect for both parties. Of course Rick had shown him the money to gain himself an advantage because he knew the landlord would regard him as a tenant he wouldn't like to lose.

He had grabbed the money up greedily and

after counting up every note to ensure it was the full amount he readily gave Rick his keys and told him if he had any problems to just contact him although Rick would not be wishing to register complaints and be coming into contact with nobody at all once he moved in.

He wondered to himself, and laughed inwardly, what the reaction of the landlord would be had he known that the money just given to him belonged to one of his community who had been strangled to death.

He doubted it would have made one bit of difference to be honest because many of these slum landlords have no scruples whatsoever and he had just managed to fill his wallet and rent out a room which normally acted as merely a storage room full of surplus mattresses and bric a brac.

He had assured Rick that the room would be empty and clean by the following Tuesday but they both knew that wouldn't happen and neither of them cared to be honest. He had his rent and Rick has his room and both were happy.

Rick would do his own cleaning and rid the room of it's excess furnishings, it had been a productive evening and he returned to his present resting place to inform Mick and Caron of the news which they were glad to hear because they had presumed he would drag his feet and be there many months yet and outstay his welcome.

It was an uncomfortable, polite silence throughout the evening and especially when Caron had disclosed that she had emptied the remainder of the wraps of heroin and its contents down the toilet and flushed them away and lectured him that she had never been as disgusted knowing that filthy drug had been used in her home.

He apologised profusely and assured them both he was not a regular user and it would not happen again, it didn't matter the heroin had gone because on the rare occasion he did use it he would have no trouble finding it once he moved into his next hall of residence. It was rife amongst them and easy to purchase.

Chapter Nine

He was up bright and early on the following morning, with the intention of having a look at the school over in Bradford where his children had purported to have been sighted.

After explaining to Mick and Caron what he intended to do they both wished him luck and were relieved he was about to do something positive with his day but Caron still wasted no time in telling him he must not bring no more drugs back with him into their home and they made plans to share a special meal that evening as a goodbye goodwill gesture.

He parked by the school and got out once it was the dinner time break and observed all of the children on the playground until such a time as a teacher approached him and demanded to know just exactly what he was doing. Rick explained without going into too much detail about his children being taken away but she seemed to have little or no sympathy as she insisted he would need to move away from the premises or she would need to notify the police which angered him considering the facts he had just given her.

A few children gathered round on their way back from their lunch breaks and listened to the conversation which became quite heated and the teacher stormed off to carry out her earlier threat to contacting the police.

Rick was incensed and of course he could appreciate the teachers concern with regards to the children's safety but he felt he had explained his situation in a reasonable manner.

He also understood her concerns that he could possibly be a peodophile lurking outside of a school and he supposed being in a van which could be used for the purpose of concealment didn't do much to help his case.

He decided to leave but not before a small boy approached and asked Rick did he say Kyle because if so he was a classmate of his and the boy went on to describe Kyle in detail and Rick had no doubt at all they were discussing his son and after hurriedly writing his mobile telephone number down on a scrap of paper he gave it to the boy to pass on to Kyle requesting him to ring him and after the boy promised to do so he drove quickly out of the area.

He parked up in a lay by to assess the situation and gather his thoughts. For all that he hadn't seen his boys it certainly didn't seem as if it had been a fruitless journey. Some good would come of it! Surely!

It wasn't as if he wanted contact with his ex partner. If she had chosen to share her mattress with another partner that was none of Ricks business and he wished her nothing but well, but it's a little harsh when the father is expected to vanish off the face of the earth as if he had never ever existed and therefore affording the recent partnership the luxury of living in a perfect little bubble with no complications.

It had all tired him out a little with the trauma of it all and he went and laid down in the back of the van to have a little power nap.

He woke, startled, with his phone ringing in his pocket and by the time he had gathered his thoughts he almost missed the call.

He wished he had done when the voice at the other end of the phone proclaimed himself to be a police officer who was giving him a friendly warning that it would be unwise to be outside of the school again or he would possibly find himself arrested.

"Are you people for fucking real" Rick screamed "arrested for what? Speaking to my own children" he told the policeman as politely as he could to leave him the fuck alone and don't ever ring his number again.

He was raging as he kicked the side of the van and infuriated that the police had dared issue him with threats but what had angered him more was being informed that Kyle had gone straight home and given the number to his mum who in turn had contacted the police.

He dreaded to think the tissue of lies the children had been told in respect of their father for Kyle to have reacted the way he did.

Although he had killed previously and been cautious about it at this moment he could kill again without thought and it was fortunate no one was in the vicinity as he kicked the back doors of the van open and jumped out like a raging bull.

He now felt betrayed by his own son and it seemed that he now had nothing left. He no longer even had that special relationship that a father enjoyed with his son.

His whole world seemed to have collapsed in on him and someone would need to pay and the way he was feeling that could only mean one thing.

Another loss of life!!

He seen no purpose in making straight back to his present home because he would be no company for anyone in this frame of mind and so he made for Dewsbury town centre to maybe do a little shopping and buy things he would need for his new home.

Retail therapy he believed the women called it although he doubted very much it would placate his mood!

He bought a few odds and ends he felt he may need and satisfied with his purchases he took a steady stroll about and without realising he found himself on the street leading towards the cafe and before he could retreat and turn and walk back the way he had entered it was too late as a uniformed constable asked him did he use this route often and had he seen anything suspicious in the previous days.

Rick remained calm and even brazenly replied that he did not even realise a cafe existed within this street and after they had both joked that it was small and easily overlooked they both said their goodbyes.

Rick had always been cool, calm and collected and thought he had handled that situation admirably and had not given no cause for concern. Even so he promised himself from now on to give that particular street a very wide berth.

He was hungry but did not wish to spoil his appetite for the special evening meal which Caron had promised so he opted for a quick snack of a cornish pasty at Greggs bakery by the bus station, and nothing ever varied here in the confines of the station. The same drunks on the same benches intimidating passengers as they alighted from their coaches and badgering them for money.

Rick sat on a bench across and his old adversary, the scotch drunk, was sitting across from him and as he took a bite from the pasty his eyes stared through the drunk who by now was staring back at Rick.

The drunk didn't know what it was but some sixth sense now told him this man was dangerous and one to be avoided and he berated himself for having caused the scene that he did a few days previous which had seemed an eternity ago now but already he had seen the man on a few occasions since and he didn't like it one bit.

He was very unnerved by his presence and would prefer to remain silent. He wasn't to know but, unfortunately, it was too late for him.

The die had been cast and his name was on it!

Rick had been through a difficult day anyway and at one stage had even been prepared to kill anyone, even in broad daylight, but already in his mind he had found the solution to his bloodlust as he looked at the alcoholic hobo and it was too late in the day now to complete the act but without a shadow of a doubt this was the one.

He had been chosen and Rick thought as victims go you were a very worthy one and you would soon be meeting your god of choice. His days were numbered!

The tramp breathed a sigh of relief as Rick walked away and reaching for his bottle of crude white cider he took a very large swig from the bottle.

Jack Soames hadn't always been a drunk. He could recall much happier times when he had owned his own flourishing business and climbed the property ladder quite quickly moving to a succession of bigger and better properties and had all of the trappings of wealth and the only thing missing to complete the deal was the addition of children which after numerous medical tests it was confirmed that he was the one unable to father any.

This had rankled deeply with his wife of many years and the relationship began to deteriorate quite quickly. She had numerous affairs and this had driven Jack into drinking quite heavily and before he knew it he had lost everything. His wife had been given the house in the divorce settlement and with no semblance of order in Jack's life the business soon collapsed and he found himself on the streets with nothing but a bottle in his hands for company and he felt very aggrieved and angry at the world and on those days when he shouted abuse to everyone he came into contact with he felt he had every right to do so.

He felt worthless most days and that his life had nothing worth living for. He had often considered taking his own life but did not have the courage to do so and he seemed destined to have a lifetime of suffering he felt.

Rick wasn't to know anything of this but on the plus side in a sick twist of fate he would become his saviour in the next few days and bring his misery to an end.

They would be meeting again very soon and perhaps it would be a blessing for Jack!

Rick had bought Mick and Caron a few leaving presents amongst his shopping. Nothing to extravagant, just a bottle of wine for Caron and aftershave for Mick by way of apology for his misdemeanours in his bedroom and they all sat down to a lavish meal delivered by the local chinese take away and a proper banquet was laid out on the table.

It was a pleasant evening with no further mention of what had brought Ricks departure about.

Even without the drug situation they would have wanted him gone eventually and so all in all it was perhaps wise he left now because his urge to kill was taking up his chain of thought much more than he would have preferred and it would be much less complicated for him to carry out these acts from the privacy of his own little retreat.

The following morning they both gathered at the door to wish him well and wave him off and even though he promised to still call and see them he knew he actually wouldn't and although they had said "yes that will be nice" they also knew that they would prefer he didn't.

In his haste to acquire alternative accommodation he hadn't paid very much attention to just how dirty and unclean this room was and after a visit to the local shops he set about scouring and disinfecting the place and never sat down until he was satisfied it was clean.

He placed all of his clothes on the hanging rail provided and found little secure hiding places within the room for his money and valuables all with the exception of the gold coins which he placed inside the plastic egg and inserted up his rectum. He had done this same exercise on many occasions down the years to escape detection from any drug squad raids or even to smuggle in on a prison visit. It would always sit comfortably once in place and would only ever need to be removed should he need to complete his toilet duties or to retrieve something from it.

That would not be necessary at this moment because all but one of the coins had been placed inside the plastic and one remained out and was being spun between Rick's fingers until it was given its chance to meet his next victim.

Rick had decided that was to be his calling card. He had not received much attention so far but by leaving a second coin he knew the cat would be released from the bag and thrown amongst the pigeons.

He wondered what tag name they would apply to the murders as he lay on the bed to go to sleep.

He quite liked the idea of being called GOLDIE!

Chapter Ten

Paula Wilcox. James O'Dowd looked down and stared at the case file in front of him on his desk.

Her name had only come to the attention of the police before because she had rang on several occasions when she had been beaten very violently by an ex - partner and it had become so regular that her seven year old daughter, Rachel had been taken into care by Dewsbury social services for her own safety.

He calculated Rachel Would be almost eleven now and after a few phone calls discovered she was happily placed with foster parents and had been for the previous three years and that her birth mother had long since broken contact.

He saw no reason to be rocking the apple cart of an eleven year old girl so asked social serves to place the details on her file for her to discover herself once she reached eighteen years of age. That's if she chose to do so.

Enquiries had been made and no other next

of kin could be found. Both parents had deceased it seemed which saved one of the uniformed officers the task of knocking someone else's door and probably ruining their lives too.

It seemed there wouldn't be many tears cried anywhere at the loss of Paula and that made James even more determined to catch her killer because he felt her life meant a sight more than the gruesome end she had endured.

He looked again at her photo and imagined her to have been a very cute child, who would have given her parents hours and hours of laughter.

What ever she had done throughout her life and whichever wrong turns she had taken she wouldn't have ever caused anyone any harm or done anyone a bad deed.

She would have been a single mum craving a little love in her life which instead turned to brutality and towards the end even felt a failure as a mother.

She had perhaps just wanted just that reassuring arm around her shoulder telling her everything was going to be ok, but instead found arms around her throat!

"I want this bastard nailing" he said to Linda Peterson and she assured him they were investigating every avenue and information was coming in by the minute of leads that would certainly need following up.

Nothing significant she had to admit but

it was all the little bits of trivia that would eventually lead to building a case.

They was of the opinion that it would soon be solved and it would be someone who had lost control of his emotions and would be so full of remorse that he would eventually even hand himself in when the guilt became too much.

They had all done as much as what they possibly could throughout the day, and after filing all of their documents and turning out all of the lights in the incidents room they all wished each other good night.

They had no idea of what was to come in the incident room and it would be the last time any of them would be going home early for a long while once the reality set in that they had a serial killer on the loose.

GOLDIE would be awake and planning his next kill while all of the murder squad were still soundly asleep in their beds.

Chapter Eleven

Rick woke early and paced up and down the room and his mind raced coming up with various plots, schemes and ruses on how to complete today's mission, but without drawing attention to himself because of the busy location his intended victim always seemed to be in.

There would be no turning back now he had awoke with the desire to kill and it would be a day of the hunter stalking his prey until such a time as he could strike.

He put a coat on with a hood in case he should ever need to conceal his features at a later stage and he could pull it up as and when it was needed.

Surely the man would be required to leave the bus station at one time or another even if it were to go to the off licence to replenish his stocks of cider for himself and his friends.

Rick did not live far from the town now and it was quite easy to just have a steady stroll down there and come back home at different intervals.

He had already done so on several occasions and had given up on encountering him on this particular day when all of a sudden, to Rick's delight, there he was sat alongside two other scruffy drunkards and being his customary insulting abusive self to anyone who walked by.

Rick went away and thought up a plan to get him away from the others while also not giving them a chance to see his face although in all honesty they were all just a little bit more than inebriated and he doubted they would ever be able to remember his face but he would rather not take the chance.

He went around the corner and bought cigarettes and two bottles of Jack Daniels whisky and made his way back around in the general direction of the station but without going in for now.

He sat on the wall across and on the odd occasion he put the bottle to his mouth and pretended to drink from it when he seen his target glancing over but each time he got a chance he would pour some of the bottle away but always given the impression that the content was getting lower.

It began to rain and Rick pulled his hood up around him and the tramp motioned for him to come and sit undercover but he declined as he wished to keep any other human contact to a minimum.

He was correct in assuming Jack would make his way over like a moth to a bulb once he realised Rick had another bottle in his pocket.

The tramp recoiled in terror upon realising the man under the hood was the very same one who had been staring at him intently the past few days until he visibly relaxed when Rick told him he had recently become homeless himself and was struggling to come to terms with it.

"You'll be struggling even more if you keep buying whisky" said Jack and laughed. Because he remembered when he, himself, first ended up on the streets and due to his previous expensive style of life his choice of poison had been brandy which he had drank for as long as he could possibly afford but his self pity now wallowed in harsh white cider.

Rick offered him the bottle which he accepted gratefully and the taste of fine whisky lingered in his mouth as it was the first expensive alcohol he had tasted for a while. He greedily drank mouthful after mouthful and only paused to return the bottle to Rick on perhaps one occasion which Rick didn't mind because he wanted him drunk and easy to over power.

The dark night had began to draw in now and his earlier drinking partners had made their way towards him ready to depart to whichever derelict house they were sleeping in that night but Jack had other ideas and didn't want his friends meeting his new ally who seemed to have money to spare.

He had jumped up and called them all the names

under the sun while continually throwing hay makers and shadow boxing like all drunken men do.

After a while of exchanging insults the other men staggered off drunkenly and went their separate ways.

He grabbed at the bottle and snatched it from Rick content that he had fought off all challengers and he was still the king of the homeless in his foolish drunken mind.

Upon emptying the bottle he threw it over the wall where it smashed into several pieces and this man was getting very drunk and would soon attract attention.

"Giz the other bottle Jimmy" he demanded in his whining scottish voice but Rick told him he always saved that to drink where he slept in the park albeit with the bait that suggested he could join him if he wanted to knowing full well he would be like a lamb to the slaughter literally!

The bottle of whisky was like waving a carrot in front of him and he reeled from pavement to pavement and could barely stand on his feet.

Rick would just need to pick his moment and find a quiet spot and this one would be his easiest victim yet and he doubted a struggle would even ensue.

The drunk had just taken yet another swig from the second bottle and after handing it back to Rick he stupidly said "hey see you ya ken.

I hope ya aren't a weeny gay"
Rick was incensed and could wait no longer and
as they rounded the next corner he brought the
bottle down in an arc like movement and broke
it against the wall.
The stupid drunk just had enough time to say
"you stupid basta, have you just dropped the
bottle, you better have another" he had wanted
to say the words but he was cut off in mid
sentence by the jagged neck of the bottle
being stuck into his throat and neck and
severing his main artery and blood spurting
everywhere but death came about very quickly
after a few body spasms.
Rick dragged him very quickly to the bushes
at the back of the park bench and there he
realised that blood had squirted over all of
his clothing and now this was a reason he was
thankful he no longer lived with Caron and
Mick.
He stood there and watched the blood drain
from him and realised he had an erection yet
again. It seemed to be that this was now Rick's
ultimate orgasm. It was a strange feeling but
he now liked it so he didn't see it stopping
anytime soon.
Now things had reached another level he
thought as he dragged the body to the back of
the benches where it was concealed by darkness
but easily discoverable at first light.
He muttered that he would have drinks to toast
Jack's demise in the morning in the tramps ear

and prepared to do one final act that he knew
would make this an whole different ball game
for all parties concerned.
He opened Jack's hand and very gently placed
a mexican gold coin in it and closed his fist
tightly.
The only good thing that had come out of this
was Jack's suffering was finally at an end.
He could rest in peace!
Rick had enjoyed this kill much more than the
previous two but he was certainly covered in
a great deal of blood and would need to keep
to the back streets on his way back to his
room.
He would need to keep in the shadows once or
twice and hide himself while people who could
be potential witnesses made their way home.
Upon arrival at his new home he rummaged
through the wheelie bin and retrieved two
plastic carrier bags to place over his feet
and delicately made his way up the stairs
careful not to disturb any other residents.
He spread a large bathroom towel on his
livingroom floor and stripped off very slowly
and carefully and placed all of his clothes
and shoes onto the towel, and wrapped them
into a tight bundle, and he would be up very
early to dispose of them in a very remote area
before the shit hit the proverbial fan which
he assumed would be very early the following
morning.
From here on it would very much be a game of

cat and mouse and he would need to tread much more carefully.

He was running with the foxes now and he knew the hounds would soon be involved in the chase and he would need to be very careful not to leave to much of a scent.

With this in mind he gathered all of his bloodied clothes together the following morning and made his way down the stairs and threw all of the knotted bundle into the back of his van.

Upon turning around he was startled to see a very pretty Muslim girl stood by the entrance smoking a cigarette, and she said "you must be the new tenant! My name is Sarita" he studied her up and down and would guess she was in her mid twenties in age but she was certainly a pretty girl and he would certainly wish to get to know her a little better.

She informed him she was running a little late and was on her way to the local university so Rick offered her a lift and he soon discovered that she was single and lived in the room below him and focused all of her time on her studies and didn't have much of a social life but occasionally she would have an evening off and relax with a few drinks indoors and said she would invite Rick around the next time she had planned to do so.

He waved her off and told her should she need a lift again to just come and knock his door. He couldn't take his eyes from her as she walked away and decided he wanted a taste of her sooner rather than later.

He turned on the radio to discover that the local news channel was relaying a story about a body being found in the local park by a dog walker and it was being treated as suspicious circumstances but no further information was available at this time.

He pulled into the next garage and filled the tank and also filled a jerry can with additional petrol and then proceeded to drive out to some very remote woodland that he knew of that he used to visit as a child.

He dragged the knotted bundle of clothes out that he had placed inside of a bin liner out and also the bag containing the wool and knitting needles which he knew he would not need again and built a bonfire, and doused everything in petrol from the can and burnt a few items at a time so as not to attract any needless attention with any excess smoke.

He need not have worried because this spot was very secluded indeed and not one person would pass giving him ample time to burn items through and also kick and scatter the ashes about and after putting a few pieces of greenery in the spot that had recently been ablaze he was satisfied that no semblance of a fire or anything untoward remained and he jumped in the van and left the site pleased with his morning work.

His killing spree had only just began and he

had no desire to be apprehended this early into what he now regarded as some sort of misguided mission.

He would now need to be much more cautious than he had ever been throughout his criminal career.

He had been a burglar and a drug dealer and all aspects of crime, he thought, involved a lot of cat and mouse tactics with whichever police department one was involved with and it was a case of avoiding detection or enduring the capture and being arrested.

But this was to be a whole different ball game! This was murder!

Some of the other menial crimes down the years that he had committed could be left on file for weeks or months at a time and could be investigated as and when.

But the chase had changed!

A murder squad would be tasked on a daily basis to solve that one particular crime and Rick had left them in no doubt now that he had killed before.

So this investigation would now exceed all others and he would be playing cat and mouse still but there would now be many more cats involved in the chase.

He certainly knew that he was the mouse and greatly outnumbered.

He would need to be box clever to stay one step ahead.

Chapter Twelve

On first appearances it looked to the uniformed police in attendance that it was maybe a fight, gone wrong, between two drunks over who should have the last drink from the bottle but having said that the injuries here in this instance were a little savage to say the least, as he stared down at the corpse by his feet.

They had cordoned the area off and now safe guarded the scene while they awaited the arrival of more senior officers than themselves.

Detective constable John Phelps was the first to arrive on the scene and he also concluded that it had perhaps been a fight amongst drunken tramps and after all possible evidence had been gathered up and placed in bags he gave permission for the body to be removed and sent to the laboratory to determine the cause of death.

It looked straight forward and a cut and dried case to him and he made his way back to the station to report his findings to his governor.

James O'Dowd had not long been at his desk and was still only on his second coffee of the day when John Phelps notified him of the incident in the park and although it seemed routine he was still a little alarmed at just how many murders were appearing to stack up.

"Not another one" he exclaimed "what the fuck is happening around here lately?"

He listened carefully to Johns possible version of events and he was happy to concur with that conclusion because he had worked with him a long time and he knew John to be a good copper and he already had him in line to replace him once he did finally retire.

He intended recommending John very strongly to fill his boots. He was already about to be promoted on James advice but he would discover that himself in a couple of weeks.

They were a good team. A strong unit and very little animosity between them down the years. He had enjoyed working with them.

His chain of thought was disturbed by the

sound of the telephone ringing on his desk and the pathologist at the other end declaring that he had "better come down here! There's something you need to see"!!

He drove there with John and upon arrival they were ushered in and Roger Dickinson, the pathologist, wasted no time in pointing to the deceased man's hand and especially the coin that lay there.

Jesus christ! James needed to sit down almost immediately and gather his thoughts but his police instincts soon went into overdrive as he informed John to notify everyone that all leave was to be cancelled and to make every officer available for a briefing in the next couple of hours.

He raced to the park area, in his car, with John and studied the area around the bench with a fine tooth comb and had it completely sealed off once again, but this time for the foreseeable future nobody would be allowed within a hundred yards of the scene.

He then went back to the incident room and instructed the officers now involved in the inquiry that under no circumstances should certain details be released to the press.

He would perhaps use them at a later stage but for now he did not wish to cause any great alarm or panic in the public domain.

This bastard had left his calling card and now he would need to study both cases in much more detail if he was to solve this quickly.

Once he began to look for similarities he quickly realised that both had incurred throat injuries and he told one of the junior officers to go and search the taxi drivers car, which was still in the pound having forensic tests, with a possibility of discovering yet another coin within it and he stressed that he wanted a very meticulous search throughout.

He despatched someone else to study all cctv footage available from both of the evenings of the murders although he realised he may have left this too late.

"Anything at all" he bellowed "find me anything"

The inevitable call came from upstairs that the superintendent wished to speak with him and before he departed he once again stressed the importance of not revealing certain details.

"God he thought! The fucking press would have a field day with this"

The super wasn't in the best of moods when james entered and left him in no doubt that these murders needed resolving and that he would expect any arrests to be imminent.

It was at times like this james wished he had taken his retirement earlier because someone would always pay the price for any shortcomings and be singled out as a scapegoat and it would never be the fat bloated bastard sat across from him.

Did he think that all of us downstairs did nothing all day? Did he not think we wanted to apprehend the killer just as quickly as he did?

The problem James had, and he knew it, was that he would now be called up on a daily basis to give him all of the updates instead of leaving him alone to do what he did best! Which was police work.

Every minute spent in here was a minute lost. He needed to be downstairs and on the frontline with his colleagues and a maniac was on the loose who they needed to detain.

He closed the door quietly as he left but on the other side of the door raised his middle finger in anger at the conversation that had just taken place.

His super talk had been more in concerns of statistics and the bad image this may portray on his force and he doubted he even gave the actual murder victims any thought at all.

James certainly did though and even with his underpaid and overworked body of men he was determined that they would all get justice. He rang his wife and told her not to expect him home anytime soon and set about going through the mass of paperwork that had accumulated on his desk.

After a while he was informed that no coin had been found in the taxi and he thought maybe he read a little bit too much into it and that it had actually been exactly what he

first thought and a drug robbery and so he
gathered all paperwork to do with that case
and place them in a completely different tray
and isolated it from others.
"The coins he shouted" i want to know exactly
where they have come from! Can someone get on
that straight away please"! He thought they
must have some sort of significance.
After first confirming that neither victim
knew each other they could now set up two
chains of enquiry and just hope for a break
quickly.
James would sit at his desk and sift through
every detail in the hope that a mistake would
be made by the killer because rest assured if
there was one James would pick up on it.
He let the others do the walking and talking.
He preferred doing his work by doing the
paperwork and instructed all of his men to
bring any detail to him no matter how trivial
it seemed.
  It was on one of these visits that a junior
colleague had dropped a few stills from a cctv
camera but it was of a very grainy nature and
they couldn't be sure it was the tramp or the
murderer. All they could be sure of was that
it was two males together and further
examination of the actual camera and the
movements of the men one of them did appear
to stagger from time to time.
A gut instinct told him that this was their
man and "yes you bastard" he thought to

himself we have our first sighting and it may not be a good one but it was what it was. An actual sighting!

He studied and studied the stills and zoomed in once or twice and he couldn't swear on oath if he was needed to but he was certain the arc of the motif on the coat represented a brand he was familiar with THE NORTH FACE and so from that he presumed the murderer was a little fashion conscious and noted that down.

It was all calculations and guess work at this time but from a few little stills he could begin to build up a picture that he was happy to go with.

He had not become a good copper overnight . he had many years of experience and was prepared to go with his judgement.

He notified his close team that he suspected they were looking for perhaps a younger sort of male and one who preferred dressing rather stylish but he readily admitted that he could also be wrong but for now to bear that information in mind whilst conducting any inquiries.

Information was coming in at a rate of knots and very quickly the paperwork was building up and the incident room was becoming a hive of activity.

It had been confirmed that the coins had been identified as the ones stolen from a burglary at the museum in Leeds. The curator was as certain as he could be that they were the exact same ones.

"Right" O'Dowd commanded "i want the names of anyone suspected of the break in on my desk within the next hour".

There was more CCTV footage to view from in and around the bus station and O'Dowd shouted to "slow that down and rewind the previous ten seconds" and there plain to see was a male wearing a grey coloured coat and no doubt about the lettering this time, because just has he had suspected earlier THE NORTH FACE stared him in the face.

"Gotcha ya bastard" but there would still be a long way to go because the suspect had his hood up and his face was indistinguishable. But even so he felt the net was closing in by the day and he now knew a little more than he did previously.

He ordered his men to trawl through all of the footage from that day in the town centre and to find him a clear image of this man's face. He mistakenly instructed them to look for the actual coat the killer was wearing and to find him in it at all costs.

Rick hadn't been foolhardy enough to wear it throughout and on most occasions he would leave it in his room or even in the van and only put it on as and when he needed to conceal his identity which wasn't an everyday habit. Only when he needed to kill!

James wasn't to know this and at this moment the importance of the enquiry would be to follow up every lead choose how trivial it appeared to be. He intended to crack this case no matter how long it took.

Detective Sergeant Williams said "i don't mean to alarm you guv but eleven coins were taken in the burglary"!

"Jesus fucking christ" thought O'Dowd "is this maniac intending to put all of them to use"?

He hoped not because he recalled the panic and alarm all throughout Yorkshire with the last infamous serial killer that was Peter Sutcliffe. The Yorkshire ripper who butchered many prostitutes and when he was finally arrested he was detained and held in the very cell block below him now.

He recalled being a junior officer at the time and lots of back slapping and high fives from everyone within the police station.

He had looked through the eye hole in the cell door and stared, chillingly, straight into the eyes of a monster and the memory had remained with him throughout his career.

Pray to god we didn't have another killer of that magnitude on their hands, he had thought.

He did not know how long he could keep the killer's "calling card" sign a secret and he would need to make that decision himself sooner or later if he ever felt that it was to the polices advantage, but right now he felt it would be much wiser to keep that information under his hat.

Last thing he wanted was wide spread panic amongst the public.

It seemed the man was local or, if not now, he had been at some stage due to his knowledge of the area.

He quickly ruled out a few of the known murderers from the town because they were still safely under lock and key but he wanted the few killers out on licence to be arrested and questioned.

Had they not been involved they may at least have heard rumours and could hold the key to this.

Most of the actions being undertaken were a shot in the dark really but the room had become a hive of activity now and this is what James really liked. The true police work that he loved to be involved with.

He had the bit between his teeth in the exact manner as a dog with his bone. Forensics contacted James to inform him that after detailed examinations of the woman's wounds they had found minute traces of wool and they were confident enough to calculate that they believed the murder weapon to have been a knitting needle.

"For god's sake" does this maniac even carry such items about with him?

Was there any significance in his choice of weapons? Did he have a partner who knitted? Did the victim knit? He had an hundred questions that needed answering. He despatched two officers to the victim's flat to see if she made any knitwear herself but this proved to be a fruitless journey as it was almost certain she did not.

So it was either a spur of the moment thing and the weapon was handy or it was pre-planned and he actually carried that on him as a weapon of choice.

They had already concluded that Paula was killed elsewhere and dumped at the spot she was found.

There had been no signs of a struggle at her home and the time of death having been established meant the four hours from her finishing work was the critical period when she encountered her killer.

James increased the police presence in the district and sent officers out doing the door to door enquiries and set about getting a few posters printed up to appeal for any information that may lead to the capture of the man.

He wanted him safely under lock and key, and hopefully before he got the opportunity to deliver the news of a third corpse to the incident room.

Chapter Thirteen

Rick soon gathered that the police presence had almost certainly increased in the town and although it had yet to be disclosed about discovery of coins on the bodies he knew, without doubt, that they were not fools and would be completely aware of the murders being linked and the need to curb his activities for the foreseeable future.

There was no rush!

He could strike again once the heat had calmed down a little. He had no inclination to make their job easy for them.

It was with this in mind he let a little sense of normality return to his life and just carried on with everyday activities and even set about finding himself a little work within the community by way of jet washing all the wheelie bins in the neighbourhood.

It gave him chance to meet some of the other

neighbours and build up a rapport with them. To any prying eyes it also gave him an image of an hard working and very industrious individual with an air of respectability about him and lessen any likely suspicions should they ever come about.

It now proved to be an ideal setting because the police very rarely ventured into any of the immigrant neighbourhoods for fear of raising any bad racial tension.

It was around this time that he became closer to Sarita and she would visit his room often and they would listen to music, get stoned and drink alcohol.

She was a practising muslim and he soon learnt that her father had been quite brutal to her until she had finally raised the courage to leave the family home. This was done with her mother's blessing as the mother could not stand to hear her daughter's screams and beatings no longer.

She had still maintained contact with her mother but obviously in a secret manner.

Rick wondered why Sarita would only come to his room and why he was never invited to hers but he never asked. He fancied her quite a lot but as of yet had not made any advances towards her because he was unsure how she would react because of her religious beliefs.

He was sure she may feel the same as he did because she greeted him warmly at the end of each working day and even though he would smell very badly due to the cleaning of the bins she would never have no hesitation in throwing her arms around him but even so they had never even actually kissed.

They would just sit in each other's company night after night and use each other as a shoulder to cry on whist they told each other of the sad incidents in their lives.

Rick would always be the one who would need to purchase the alcohol at the local shop because of Sarita's religious status and alcohol being forbidden.

She was a westernised girl though and readily accepted the culture.

It was very rare she would be seen on the estate and preferred being very reclusive and just go to her schooling or remain in her room.

Rick was just the release she had needed for a long time but she could not understand why he never attempted to kiss her or make advances.

"Perhaps she wasn't pretty enough" she thought.

Her father had told her often enough that she was ugly so she resigned herself to the fact she was not worthy of having love or finding a boyfriend.

She cared little about it for now because she was happy in his company after all the long lonely nights alone and if this was all there was to come of it then it would certainly suffice.

Such is life and she was easily pleased. Rick would always laugh when she reeled drunkenly down stairs to her own room at the end of the evening but in reality she would be imploring him to call her back.

Rick was slowly but surely falling in love with her and night after night he would wish that she simply took off her clothes and proclaimed that she was staying for the night.

They were both complex souls who had both had their share of problems and had hit that stage were neither knew what to do to create romance.

To complicate matters they could not be seen in and around the neighbourhood together or this would certainly be frowned upon and on the odd occasions they had gone out they would set of separately and meet upon the outskirts.

Sarita could never be sighted in any public house so Rick had purchased a small hip flask for her to have a sneaky little drink when the opportunity arose.

She wasn't an alcoholic or anything remotely resembling that. He just felt and she knew the same that a little alcohol would make her open up far more and relax her inhibitions and they would both be able to talk freely.

They would travel out to remote beauty spots were neither of them were known and be much more visibly relaxed and she would link her arm through his and rest her head against his shoulder.

Rick would feel good and positively glow at these moments and he wanted them to always be here.

When they had gone out on one particular day Rick took hold of her hand and as if it was the most natural thing in the world he placed a ring on her finger and declared it to be a token of their friendship.

He had used the word friend for fear of any rejection and causing offence. She smiled and accepted it gratefully and gave him a kiss on the cheek as she was unsure how to react in any other way.

Damn you! She thought. Why did you have to use that word. But even so it brought a smile to her face for the rest of the day and made her feel very special.

She would not have felt that way had she known the ring once belonged to a girl called Paula!

Who was now deceased!!

They spent a pleasant day walking around and at one time as they watched a few young boys fishing on the riverbank she casually slipped her hand into his and entwined their fingers.

She had never felt this happy but she was also aware of all of the complications this could create and she was not only fearful for her own safety but Rick's also.

They were both loathe to return home but both knew they must do so and once again part company before they reached the shared home.

He would have suggested they lay on a blanket in the back of the van but he had been having the odd recurring nightmare of what had taken place in there and anyway if anything was ever going to take place between them he would prefer a much more romantic setting than the one that offered.

They made their separate ways back and arranged to meet in his room later that night.

When she arrived later that evening he was completely took back by the effort she had obviously made because she looked a completely different girl with curves he had been unable to see on previous visits.

Sarita had set her stall out after one last lingering look in the mirror had convinced herself he must find her appealing or it would be the final time she would try.

Rick could not take his eyes from her and she knew by his reaction that she had made the right decision in her choice of clothes.

As was often the case the night would consist of small talk and both of them taking it in turns to make a joint of cannabis.

Once they were comfortably stoned and clumsy with it Rick reached out for an ashtray and both of their legs brushed together and after an awkward giggle and little eye contact the moment had finally arrived and Rick arched his head to make contact with her mouth for the first time.

She accepted him willingly and encouraged him further by sticking her tongue into his mouth.

It was as if all of their demons had been released and they devoured each other hungrily.

No words needed to be spoken until they both collapsed into each other's arms totally spent and exhausted.

They both clambered into bed and embraced each other tightly only stopping to laugh at both their revelations that they had wanted to do this long before they had.

But the barriers were down now and the floodgates opened, literally, as they began to repeat the love making of earlier.

Finally they both fell to sleep and Sarita used Rick's chest as a pillow. He awoke to see her gathering up her clothes to get dressed in the corner of the room and he marvelled at what a superb figure she had. He watched, admiringly, without letting her know he was awake until he could finally hold it no longer.

"Morning gorgeous" he said. Upon realising he had stirred she ran across to the bed and gave him the biggest kiss he could wish for.

They had both certainly given each other mixed signals but for sure they would be catching up on any lost time now the ice had finally been broken.

He even felt confident enough to pat one of her lovely firm buttoks and wish her a good day of learning as she hurried out the door already running late.

She assured him it was ok and she didn't require a lift and blew him a flurry of kisses as she left.

"Wow" he thought "what a mind blowing night" and he promised himself that he wanted many more of them.

He showered and felt a new man and decided to take the day off work. He was his own boss so why not? He was answerable to nobody. He felt really content that he and Sarita were now appearing to be an item.

He was love struck and even this early in the day he already missed her and could not wait for her to return.

He was elated and he wanted to tell the whole world about her but he knew he could not do so within their own community.

But he was bursting to tell someone and decided to have a steady walk down to see Caron and Mick to at least tell someone his good news.

It was a nice enough day and he chose to walk rather than drive and he simply floated along he was that euphoric and he had that added spring in his step that any new romance brings about.

He was in a world of his own as he took the shortcut through the park and before he knew it found himself stood alongside the very bench that was the scene of the tramps murder. Far from being reviled as could be expected he found himself to be very sexually aroused and to the extent that he entered the bushes and masturbated himself furiously as every single detail of the night flashed through his head while all the time stimulating him more. He ejaculted two or three times and then adjusted his clothing to make himself presentable and exited at a different point of entry.

That was the first time he had even thought about the murders for a while and it surprised him how he had reacted.

There was an ice cream parlour within the confines of the park and he sat on one of the tables outside while he ate his ice cream. He almost choked on it when in the distance he seen a uniformed policeman approaching.

"Good morning sir! Sorry to trouble you!" he then asked Rick did he use the park often? Had he been there on a particular occasion when someone had been murdered? Had he ever noticed anything unusual.

He thought he was never going to go away but after Rick assured him it was very rare he used the park the constable just ambled away wishing him a good day and, smilingly, told him to enjoy his ice cream.

Rick felt a little unnerved but felt he had handled the situation with aplomb.

It was just routine, plain and simple nothing to bring about alarm. It was just a beat bobby going through the motions until the end of his shift.

Hadn't the Yorkshire ripper been spoken to many times before he had actually been arrested.

Remain calm and collected is the best form of defence.

But even so he decided that in future stay away from the park or any of his murder scenes come to that.

He decided not to bother going to visit Caron and Mick.

The constable had flustered him enough to make him retreat to the safety of his living room.

Chapter Fourteen

The super left instructions for o'dowd to come up to his office.
"Here we fucking go" he thought and had every intention of telling him that rome wasn't built in a day but in his heart he knew he wouldn't have the courage to tell him so.

Upon entering he was introduced to a well dressed man absolutely reeking of some sort of expensive designer aftershave and informed his name was Detective Inspector Graham Albrighton and that he would be working alongside him but o'dowd thought it was a polite way of saying that he would now no longer be in charge of the investigation.
He shook his hand albeit only out of politeness because he knew this latest recruit was set to undermine his authority and

he knew that all of his team would see it in the same way.

O'Dowd was told that the officer had been involved in a spate of linked murders in the South East Region of the UK and due to his success in solving that case he had now been seconded to this unit to give us the benefit of his knowledge and experience.

"Why thank you superintendent" he thought. That makes me feel a whole lot better about my own capabilities and also that of my team. He was told to take him downstairs and give him access to all areas and fill him in on any progress IF ANY had been made.

He was infuriated at the term "IF ANY" but he chose to bite his lip. Did he think they had all been sat having the odd hand of poker for the past few weeks or something?

He found his words very disrespectful and the sooner he retired and no longer worked for this man the better.

As expected the introduction of the new man did not go down too well and one or two were confused as to who they should report any information to.

O dowd went to pour himself a glass of whisky from his cabinet before realising that his new ally was observing and when he declared quite smarmily "Not for me Sir!" then O,dowd chose himself not to have one.

Oh it was going to be fun having this one around he thought as he winked at Linda

Peterson.

Already with barely a word spoken o'dowd had calculated that Graham "Mister almighty" Albrighton was the new head of office and he was making that quite clear now the formalities were out of the way.

He made his way to the coffee machine rather than having a whisky and when he returned the new kid on the block was even sat at his desk and leafing through the paperwork that had been highlighted as "Of Importance"

Maybe he should drink his coffee, order a taxi, go home and light his pipe and put his slippers on, thought O,dowd

He did not have the effort to even try and make things comfortable with this man. Battle lines had already been drawn and he knew there wasn't a hope in heaven of them working alongside each other in a compatible manner .

He was a typical southerner. A proper 'Flash Harry' and he had already noticed him giving Linda's backside a friendly pat as she walked by his desk and it wasn't as if Linda had been in the least bit offended so in the space of a few hours O'Dowd was set to lose his superior authority, his desk and now even his ex mistress to the new sheriff smelling of David Beckham or whatever brand of aftershave it was.

God he hated the man already , the whole office stank of his presence . He called everyone together for the informal introduction to explain who the new man was and his rank but he had barely begun before albrighton said I will take over from here and give more details than you actually know James but thank you anyway.

This bastard was making it very clear for all to see who was running the show now. The head honcho had spoken and everyone had better listen was the impression he was giving out and complete silence fell over the room.

O'Dowd stood there like a spare part and was not invited or encouraged to speak so he did not do so. "Well I think that went well" claimed Albrighton and now let's find ourselves a killer he added like it was the easiest thing in the world.

What had started as a mutual consultation between the pair fizzled out to be a one man show as albrighton practically bullied his way to the head of affairs.

O'Dowd just stepped aside meekly because at his time of life he couldn't be arsed with additional drama and although he would rather the case be solved he could always have the satisfaction of watching "flash harry" come out of it with egg on his face and his pride hurt if the case were not to be solved.

He issued instructions to some of the team to follow up this or that certain lead and they were given no opportunity to say that someone was already covering that before he moved onto

someone   else   barking   out   further
instructions.

They were bemused and looked towards
O'Dowd but he simply shrugged his shoulders
and sat down to go through his own papers and
distanced himself from all of the proceedings
taking place. If he wished to assume command
then let him do so while he went quietly about
his own work.

The lunatics have taken over the asylum
he laughed inwardly.
He noticed he had kept Linda free to work
alongside of him and he promised to warn her
of the possibility that he may be married and
to tread careful but she would perhaps see
that as a sign of his own jealousy so decided
to let them both dig each other into any holes
of their own making.

He was glad when the shift had ended and
readily agreed with anyone who would care to
listen that he had just worked one of the most
awkward days he had ever had as a working
police officer.

He was determined to solve the case
himself and not just for the glory but also
to get rid of this young pretender as soon as
he possibly could and for that reason alone
he would do something he had never done
before. He would take as many documents as it
was possible to carry with him to his home each
night once he had photocopied them. He would
work alone at home each night and do so in

comfort and under no pressure.

Something he doubted Albrighton would do. He pictured him quaffing cocktails at some hotel bar whilst all the while impressing the ladies by producing his warrant card and offering them a night in his hotel room …. With handcuffs of course!!

The quicker we waved this one off back to London would be better for all concerned he thought to himself.

He never discussed work with his wife but she could tell he was in a mood over something and thought it unwise to ask and so after making him yet another coffee that he would probably let go cold and gently kissing him on the head she wished him goodnight and told him not to work too late.

He perused the papers over and over until they gave him a headache but still failed to find any clue that would lead to the man's capture. He retired for the night and planned to be up and about early and in the office each day long before Albrighton, not that it was a competition between them he just always done it to maintain standards amongst his team.

He was classed as the leader as regards to morale and he had always set the standard and led by example and that was not about to change now. The older he had now become meant he slept less hours anyway which made the task much easier anyway.

Flash Harry would obviously turn up

smelling of his aftershave and possibly his early morning martinis or whatever he had partaken in at the bar. It was not the lifestyle O'Dowd even contemplated, he would be much happier having his late night bedtime night cap and show up at his work place bright eyed and bushy tailed.

He had reached the rank that he had by being a very diligent officer throughout his career and resented very much that this man had acquired the same status in half the time perhaps on the back of a few lucky breaks or more likely off the back of someone else's good police work.

The following morning as he arrived at work there was a little unrest among the men who insisted they prefered being under his command and had become confused by recent events. O'dowd assured them that he was still always available to confide in but for the meantime just to go with the flow of things . He was glad he still had the support of his team and why not because they had worked alongside each other for many years.

When Albrighton arrived and realised there had been no further developments he announced he wished to visit both of the murder scenes and so O Dowd agreed to accompany him which proved to be an awkward journey with many uncomfortable silences. So what did he expect he would find so long after the events and what a fully experienced forensic team hadn't?

It was as if he was questioning the professionalism of the entire police force, or maybe he simply needed a spell out in the fresh air to help sober him up a little bit he thought jokingly.

He then wished to be taken to where the other drunks usually gathered and to ask had they seen anything unusual on the day of the murders or the days leading up to them.
A very shabby dressed man with a scruffy beard informed him that they had already been asked these very same questions and had in fact made statements.

Albrighton chose to ignore him and asked yet another question and O'Dowd was now becoming a little embarrassed to be in his company.

God how James needed a whisky he thought while he noticed one of the tramps had a bottle in his hand but he knew that once they got back to the incident room it would be the last thing he would consider because some sixth sense told him that Albrighton would have been instructed to come up and see the super at anytime he wished to do so throughout his stay and he did not wish to give him the opportunity to mention his drinking habits.

Obviously some had been impressed by him because he had not seen Linda with this much makeup or attention for a long while and wasn't the only one to notice because some other members of the team were having a sneaky giggle in case she was making herself appear a fool by dressing up. It was in this setting police work and murder investigations were meant to be taking place. "God help us" he thought although he knew he could definitely rely on the core of his team to not be distracted.

It was business as usual for the murder squad.

Their noses were to the ground looking for the scent.

The hunt was on again.

Chapter Fifteen

Rick would safely say this was the best period of his life and was up there with the birth of his children.
He was never looking for love but he had found it with Sarita . Even allowing for the fact that they couldn't go public on the relationship as it would be frowned upon and he knew her parents would never welcome him into the family fold.

Each time they were outdoors they would need to leave the area more often than not so as not to be sighted together and the relationship was fraught with tension.
Even if they went to the local cinema they would go in separately and only sit alongside each other once the lights went down and part a few moments before the end of the film.

He understood her concerns and rightly so because hadn't he listened long and hard about her father's brutality and he definitely wasn't likely to approve at all about this present situation.

He had often told her of his childhood visits to the north coast and in particular the caravan sites along the cliff tops of Flamborough bay and she suggested they both go away together and stay in one of the caravans and have a holiday, just take themselves out of their dilemma.

He readily agreed and gave her his bank card to do all of the booking when she attended her college next and had access to the computers internet.

He kissed her passionately one day as she left but failed to notice the pakistani man who had just exited the shared kitchen area carrying his breakfast on a tray.

He would live to regret that moment but for now he went back into his room and after showering he did his usual toilet routine after forcing the plastic egg out of his rectum….

He washed the egg under the tap and dried it with tissue and it had been a while since he had sat and caressed the coins but now passed them from hand to hand lovingly and wished he could have found a buyer at the time who would have given him their full worth and himself and Sarita could have used the proceeds to set up a new life away from here.

There were nine coins left and it sent a chill down his spine thinking that he may have

murdered another nine random strangers.
He was thankful that Sarita had come into his
life because he wanted to stop what he was
doing but previously couldn't find a reason
to do so.

He had been like a runaway train but she
had brought out his softer natured side and
he could not imagine himself ever killing
anyone again.
It was with this in mind that he went to a
very secluded wooded area he used to frequent
when playing truant from school and found the
familiar old oak tree with the large knothole
in it and after scaling up the tree he secreted
the egg, he had now sealed with elastoplast,
deep inside the hole and only he would know
of it's presence.

They had used this hole many times as
children to hide small items they had
shoplifted that they did not wish to take home
for their parents to discover.
He had hoped he could now put this period of
his life behind him and escape detection from
his previous misdemeanours. A sort of early
retirement and he knew the police would
eventually shelve the case and go back to
other duties. Because, after all, he was
confident he had made no mistakes and left no
clues as far as he was aware.
He was now glad he hadn't foolheartedly placed
a gold coin in the offerings box when he had
attended the confessional booth because he

had intended to do so.

Maybe at that time with a little bit of guilt and feeling remorse he had wanted to proffer the coin with the other alms as a way of getting caught.

He didn't really know why he had the urge to put one in there , all he knew was he was glad he had not done so because maybe one day the police may reveal that information to the media and he was thankful that the remaining coins were now concealed safely and hopefully never see the light of day again.

Plans had been made and that coming weekend they would both be travelling by train to their first holiday together.

They would need to make a few changes at a few stations to make the other connections but they finally arrived at the site. Got the keys to their caravan home for the next week, unpacked and Sarita just skipped and danced about like one of the actresses dancing on broken glass in a bollywood movie.

"God she was beautiful" thought Rick as he laid back in the reclining chair and marveled about just how much more visibly relaxed she was now she was away from all the prying eyes. She straddled him on the chair and about squeezed the life out of him her embrace was that tight and in that one moment alone he knew they had made the correct decision to come away for this holiday.

They could hold hands or kiss in public with
no fear of reprisals and they were like two
children playing   as   they   would   stick
ice-cream cones in each others faces and just
prance about and frolic from the dawning of
each day until sunset.

He lost count of just how many times they made
love throughout the week they done it that
often and it was plain to see a great burden
had been lifted from each of their shoulders.
They would walk all along the coastline with
it's sandy beach, often barefoot and gather
shells that sarita would place to her ear and
it was as if she had returned back to her
childhood she was so exhilarated.

After most of the walks they would always
scale the paths that led to the cliff top and
make for the one little spot they had named
"Their seat" and there they would both angle
their bare feet over the edge after carefully
placing their shoes and socks behind them.

It was a sheer drop and they would often tease
each other with gentle nudges towards the drop
but always stopping before they went too far
and usually just falling backwards and laying
there kissing each other passionately.

The odd dog walker would maybe amble past
but it was more often than not very quiet and
private. They would lay there and watch and
listen to the waves crashing into the bottom
of the cliff as the tide came in and it was
the perfect setting for them to completely

cement their love for each other.

She made him promise to always bring her here year after year She had fallen in love with not only the area but also Rick, although how she could ever say this to her family would deeply trouble her. "If we're ever apart this is where I will expect to come and find you" Sarita said. Although he thought it a strange thing to say before he could utter a response she had already begun to kiss him passionately yet again.

He went with the moment instead and soon forgot what she had said. He did not wish to get involved in any deep seated emotion and he had long since got used to Saritas ramblings anyway and he loved her no matter what and who cared if she had a troubled mind! "He was there to comfort her now" he thought as he placed his hand on her head and began to stroke her hair.

Throughout the week they would visit all of the other seaside resorts along that coastline Scarborough, Bridlington and Filey and it was a joy for him to be able to observe her drink alcohol freely in the different public houses they visited without fearing any recriminations from anyone. She was her own free spirit and a totally different girl.

God how he hated religion and all of the complications it brought about. He had been brought up as a practising catholic but the only time in recent years he had attended any church service was when he was being held in prison and that wouldn't be seeking redemption.

It would simply afford him the opportunity to get out of his cell for an hour on a sunday morning and a prison mass would always be a very well attended congregation but everyone attending would be doing so for the exact same reason which would usually be to exchange contraband. But Saritas religion, Islam, would be a very demanding religion and hadn't he even told her on more than one occasion that he was prepared to convert but she had laughed and said that it wasn't that simple and her family would still not approve.

He cursed Islam and all it represented but was determined for none of it to spoil their holiday.

He wished he could make it all go away but he had no magic wand or even the slightest solution to the problem. He knew she shouldn't be engaging in sexual activity and he would protect her at all costs and never reveal what had taken place between them. She would be at risk of beatings from her father if he discovered that she took drugs or alcohol but the stigma and shame that went with any sexual dishonour could even endanger her life the way that some Muslim parents reacted.

The only logical solution would be for them to run away at some stage and for her to change her name but even that could prove difficult if they went to the wrong vicinity because muslim immigrants had huge populations now all throughout the UK and many of them closely related by blood in some shape or form.

They both wished they could live here for all time and that the holiday would never and they had enjoyed their stay that much . The routine would never vary no matter where they had been during the day and they would both always find themselves bare footed and swinging their legs over the cliff edge with an arm around each other.

 They would see very little of the interior of the caravan and would only use it to actually sleep in at the end of the day's pursuits.

The intention of the holiday was basically to socialise together much more and they had certainly done that throughout their stay. She had laughed when he had told her of competitions that would be held such as knobby knees because she was unsure whether he was teasing her and making it up but he told her that should they hold a competition for the happiest couple on the site they would win it by a country mile.

Everyone would greet them warmly each day and smile and exchange pleasantries and how he wished everyone in the world could disregard race , creed , religion and just be kind natured to each other. In that short space of time since meeting her he had gone from being a murderous maniac to the completely opposite side of the spectrum and the only thoughts he had now were full of love.

As the holiday neared completion Sarita had only one last request she needed Rick to fulfil and he was intrigued as she led him by the hand insisting he remain barefooted and walked the mile or so to the place they had spent so many wonderful hours and engaged in much deep and meaningful dialogue and it was there she insisted that he take her, under the cover of darkness, on their favourite spot upon the cliff's edge.

She accepted him willingly as they both tore at each other under the throes of passion, neither of them could be expected to know that this was to be the final time they would make love and in the coming days they would be torn apart by matters out of their control.

Chapter Sixteen

O'Dowd now had more than enough time to peruse
through every single file and piece of paper
on his desk and he did so over and over
ensuring he had not missed that one vital clue
that would lead to the killer's capture.

Months passed and the trail had gone very
cold and the killings had stopped almost as
soon as they had started. O'Dowd would watch
hour after hour of CCTV footage and he felt
the killer was one clever devious bastard or
he very much had luck on his side thus far.
The teams hours were reduced and some of the
uniformed officers even placed back on other
duties with the backlog of crime that had
built up.

No stone had been unturned but it had
reached the stage where just a small elite
squad could now deal with any of the
information coming in.
He leafed through a few of the recent
documents and read a detailed statement from
one of the bus drivers in which he described
a verbal confrontation with the tramp that was

murdered but he couldn't really place a day
or date to the outburst because he witnessed
lots of similar incidents with the towns
drunks in the bus station on a daily basis,
but he said for some strange reason this
altercation stood out more than previous ones
and he could recall feeling thankful that he
had reached the safe sanctuary of the cab on
his bus.

Even his description of the man left a lot
to be desired and he could not safely say the
man lived locally and he had seen him on other
occasions. James felt certain that all of the
events of this day were somehow linked to the
murder. Call it what you may, "a Coppers
instinct" or "a nose for the job" but he would
need to prove it and it's what kept him up late
at night searching for the missing link.
Whilst at work he mainly worked alone anyway
because Albrighton and Linda Peterson had
long since formed a work and play partnership
but both would find it difficult to separate
one from the other and they could often be
heard playfully giggling instead of being
professional in the office.
In his opinion Albrighton had very much
outstayed his welcome and now that the
investigation seemed to be winding down he
could not understand why he had not been
issued with his return ticket home. He had no
objection at all to them having a relationship
but he very much objected to it if it affected

their police work.

He seemed to be doing his own work and theirs also at times but at least it kept him busy and gave him something to focus on.
Sergeant Williams and Constable John Phelps would be the ones he could rely on at this time while the romantic couple would take late lunches.
They showed less and less interest in the case and just went through the motions. He saw no sense in going upstairs to complain because he felt it would be simply seen as a bitter rivalry had developed.

It was beneficial really to see less and less of them because him and his two colleagues could work much more in harmony when the other pair were not about, they would discuss every angle and try to calculate did the murderer possibly live local or why had it suddenly stopped did he work away, was he in prison, did he have a family?
They tried to build a photofit and calculate an age and background.
On one of the grainier cctv stills they had been given the slightest glimpses of a fraction of his face and gathered that he was a white male but until they could actually prove this was the actual killer they did not wish to jump to conclusions because the footage they had studied may at some point be ruled out.

Not all paperwork had been dismissed but

it had been generally decided which was deemed trivial, of moderate or significant importance and was there to be accessed for any future enquiries. The three of them had always had a good police ethic about them and a good bond. They would have a few beers together on the odd occasion after work and especially if they had matters to discuss relating to the case.

Some people prefer leaving their work load back at the office upon completion of the day's shift but good coppers don't seem to do that and have a hunger, a desire, to solve outstanding crimes.

If the murderer was going to ever be apprehended then these were the three that would bring that about, the hunt and the chase would resume with the dawn of each day but the one thing that was certain was the chase would never end.

The killer would need to be cautious and not leave any scent!

Chapter Seventeen

Rick and Sarita arrived back home after an
arduous journey which seemed to take forever
which often seems the case on anyone's return
journeys. Rick supposed it's because everyone
feels the same and is loathe for the holiday
to end.

They had returned under the cover of
darkness so as not to be seen with each other
and Sarita entered the property first and was
very alarmed to discover extensive damage to
the door to her flat. She knew instantly who
it would be but preferred not to even inform
Rick of the damage so she kissed him on the
cheek as he passed and informed him she
wouldn't be coming up to his room that night
as she felt really tired with the travelling
they just done.
Once Rick was out of sight she patched the door

up as best she could and sat in the chair feeling very fearful of any further developments. Nobody could have possibly wished to do this and not even steal a single item so it was obvious to her that the only two possible culprits that it could be was her two brothers who were very much of the same ilk as her father and very nasty minded individuals who she knew would return and she was very afraid of the present situation and she laid on the bed but knew it would prove difficult to sleep.

Meanwhile upstairs Rick showered and changed his clothes then reflected on all that had taken place throughout the holiday and it gave him a pleasing glow within himself although he was a little confused as to why she did not wish to come up to his tonight. Surely she was not having second thoughts? He doubted that very much, after all of the words of love they had expressed to each other through the week away. He was stirred from his thoughts by a noisy disturbance taking place on the landing below and rushed headlong from his room to investigate.

He could hear Saritas screams and he now took the stairs two and three at a time and demanded to know what was occurring to the two bulky men on the threshold of Saritas flat. She tried to assure him everything was okay and her eyes pleaded with him not to get involved and to go back to his room.

He was clubbed to the floor with a few strikes from a baseball bat and the last thing he could recall before losing consciousness was Sarita screaming for him to be left alone. It was a while before he came round and he wasn't sure if any of his limbs had been broken because he felt unable to move in a sort of a paralysed state.

It took a while to register that he was in fact tied and secured to a chair with masking tape around his mouth.

"Who were these men? what have I done? Where is Sarita?" a thousand questions and he had no idea of the answers to any of them.

Hours seemed to have passed but was probably only minutes but finally the door opened to this very sparsely furnished room and there stood the two protagonists from the previous evening's assault and they certainly had not arrived with the intention of being friendly as he received a very firm punch to the side of the head.

The tape was ripped from his mouth but even so he felt it would be futile to make any loud pleas for help, he felt sure that they had done this same procedure at other times and any screams would fall on deaf ears.

It was to be a full blooded interrogation with the occasional slap, kick or punch for added effect and they wanted to know all about what had been taking place with him and their sister!

He knew he needed to protect her at all costs and denied time after time that anything sexual had taken place. Each time he foolishly asked if she was safe and could he see her, the beating would increase.

They would assure him that she was no longer his concern and it was very unlikely he would ever be seeing her again.

They seemed to sense that he thought that she had been killed by them saying that he would never see her again and they laughed in his face and told him they meant she had been sent away and very much in disgrace and shame. But they also informed him that he should not think his own life was safe if he did not reveal all of what they wished to know.

They told him they had killed before and would have no hesitation in doing so again . He must have looked a sorry sight to the assailants who would not have even been able to imagine that Rick was also capable of killing.

They bombarded him with questions and demanded to know every detail of the romance but Rick remained insistent that they were just good friends who resided in the same house and each time they were not happy about the reply to a question he would find himself being hit about the head and beaten again.

He had no way of knowing just how badly he looked but Rick had one of his eyes almost shut with bruising and the eyebrow on his other one would require several stitches.

A temporary respite came when someone knocked the locked door wishing to enter, a hood was placed over Rick's head and all he could hear was three voices now talking in their native tongue and as he listened closely he quickly realised one of the voices was that of an older person so he presumed this to be the father, surely the father would not condone the excessive violence being meted out although he quickly dismissed that thought when his shins were both kicked very forcefully and the older voice uttered the word "Bastard" as he left the room.

Both of the brothers would take it in turns circling the chair where Rick sat and on some laps nothing would happen but on others, when it was least expected, a full blooded punch would take place.
He was totally helpless and saw no sign of this ending and in actual fact the one thing that concerned him more than any beating was what would be the conclusion to it all.

These two unsavoury characters could be capable of anything and it wouldn't even surprise him if they had their own sister tied to a chair in another room although he doubted the father would give them permission to go that far.
Rick could taste blood in his mouth and was having difficulty replying to questions but they would see his silence as an admission of guilt. This was an absolutely dire position

to be in but he promised himself to remain strong and protect Saritas honour. He was more than confident that she would have said little or nothing because the consequences for her would be very severe.

"Explain!" One of them demanded as he put the face of Rick's phone in front of him and their words of love and devotion on a few text messages stared straight back at him.

He knew sanita always deleted hers after she had read them and it always puzzled him why but he now fully understood with the family she had to answer to.

Rick cursed himself for having saved the odd romantic one but he used to enjoy reading them over and over at any of the times they were apart.

The evidence was plain to see there before him and the only thing he could be thankful for was that none of the messages indicated anything sexual had taken place. If that had been the case he felt sure they would have cut his throat by now but even so it wasn't as if his predicament was going to lessen anytime soon.

They both left the room and Rick presumed they had gone to consult with the father about the latest developments now they had unlocked the phone and accessed all of the details.

He focused all of his energy to attempt to recall exactly which messages he had saved because he would need to be prepared for the

inevitable next round of interrogation. When
they finally returned the expected beating
never materialised and Rick was at a loss to
explain this.

They even seemed to be talking to him in a much
more softer and gentle tone and even informed
him they were going to give him a little
something to take away the pain.

He couldn't understand this different
approach all of a sudden and it had certainly
caught him off guard. He was startled a little
when he felt something tighten around the top
of his arm and before the realisation of what
was about to happen sank in he felt the sharp
prick in the lower part of his arm and the
surge of what passed through the syringe and
into his body almost took his breath away.
He had taken heroin before and had no doubt
at all what had just been injected into him
as his head slumped back into the chair and
he entered into a dream like state!

Although it relieved his pain a little he
was concerned about the intentions behind it
all because no way would this pair be doing
this with any degree of compassion towards him
and he was bemused.

He was thankful they had removed the tape
from around his mouth because he would find
himself vomiting at regular intervals due to
the purity of the heroin. He had lost track
of how many days he had been in this room as
night followed day and by now he would almost

implore the door to open.

In the early part of his captivity he would have been happy to never lay eyes on this pair again but now his eyes would stare eagerly at the door because he would be craving his next shot of heroin and his captors would recognise and tease him mercilessly.

On the occasions they did bring any drugs with them they would sit alongside Rick and ask him more questions albeit in a friendlier approach.

They had done what they had set out to do and Rick was now very much addicted and they felt it would make him confess readily to acquire that next fix but he was made of sterner stuff than that and his reluctance to impart any information had begun to convince them that perhaps there was none to give.

When they returned on one occasion they had with them a large man who blocked out the light from the hall he was that big and he strode across the room and without any hesitation struck Rick so forcefully that he and the chair fell over backwards and as he lay there helpless the man stamped heavily on his face resulting in a broken eye socket.

He did not need to think too hard to realise this was Sarita's father who did not seem to mind me witnessing his face this time. Did this mean they were going to kill him? Rick thought

But even the sons were taken back with the ferocity of the attack as they struggled to pull him away.

He decided very quickly that he would much rather endure both of the brothers beatings than the fathers. Rick now fully understood exactly what Sarita used to tell him of the tales concerning her father's brutal ways. Rick had only seen or heard him in the room twice and he wasn't looking forward to a third meeting or he doubted that he would survive it.

Even the brothers may have been thinking the exact same thing because they had given Rick an indication that he would be getting taken outside sometime soon and to be getting some fresh air.

They left the room but he could hear them both having a heated debate at the other side of the door.

One of them came back and placed the hood over his head and untied his bonds but not before warning him that should he attempt to escape it would be his undoing.

The hood was just a precaution so that Rick would never be able to identify where he had been held, he was manhandled into the back of a van and Rick was unsure of his destiny and then rather surprisingly one of his captors asked if he would like some heroin .

He was concerned about the sudden seemingly acts of kindness and he convinced himself they may wish to have him in a drug induced state before they disposed of his body.

They made a phone call and a meeting place was decided because they informed Rick they did not have any but that they had money to do so and insisted he would be the one needing to get out and do the purchase after assuring him they had a gun and if he chose to run a bullet would have his name on.

He had no reason to doubt one word they told him and anyway he was really desperate for a fix. He was given the money and pointed towards a stranger outside a telephone kiosk and after the deal was concluded he hurried back to the confines of the van and one of the brothers passed him a new syringe and informed him it was now time for him to do the procedure himself.

What Rick didn't know was that the purchase and now the act had been secretly filmed on a mobile phone to confirm that Rick was now very much a using addict and this evidence would be presented to Sarita at the earliest opportunity with the hope of convincing her that he had always been a user.

They seen it as a possible way and means of keeping them apart and this had been the objective from the very first day they had injected him.

Once the drug had yet again took a good hold of Rick and he was very disorientated, the brothers moved to the next stage of their plan.

They picked their moment carefully when little or no traffic was about, accelerated to the car park of the local hospital and threw Rick out of the van and left him there in his bruised and battered state, incoherent. and with a needle still hanging from his arm.

Chapter Eighteen

Rick came around but could barely move as he opened his eyes, very wearily, feeling very battered and bruised and attempted to ascertain exactly where he was.

He quickly closed his eyes once he realised he had uniformed police officers stood alongside where he lay.

Why were they in attendance? Was he under arrest? Would it be to do with the murders?

He tried to recall what had previously taken place to find himself in any of this predicament and decided the best bet for now would to give the impression he was still sedated until he could gather his thoughts.

He heard one of the officers speak to the nurse in attendance and it was obvious they knew his name and he assumed his pockets would have been emptied upon his arrival to confirm his identity and he was now very thankful indeed that the gold coins were not about his person and so he relaxed a little.

Once they left the room he opened his eyes a little and immediately began to engage in conversation with the nurse and it was a great relief to him to learn that in actual fact he was the victim and the police simply wanted to speak to him about how he had incurred his injuries.

She motioned to go and inform the two officers he was finally awake but Rick implored her not to do so just yet as he felt very nauseous and not quite up to any demanding questions.

He quickly realised he was hooked up to a series of drips and could now feel the uncomfortable pain that goes with a needle in the back of the hand.

He was very agitated and obviously in need of yet another fix of heroin but he could ask the nurse as often as he cared to but he doubted very much that would be freely available and provided by whichever hospital he was in.

He looked about the room because he needed to be aware of exactly where his clothes were because when the first opportunity presented itself he would be making for the nearest exit. He felt in a lot of pain though and was not quite ready to decamp yet.

He sat up rather dizzily and swung his legs over the side of the bed but did not quite have the strength to stand on his feet but he looked at his swollen features on the shiny surface of the medication trolley by his bed and he was horrified at the state of his face and everything came flooding back into his memory of the beatings and being held captive.

"Hello sir! We would like to ask you a few questions if you feel up to it" said one of the officers.

Numerous things were put to rick but he continually said he had no recollection of what had actually happened or who the assailants were.

When one of the doctors entered he brought conclusions to an end and claimed his patient needed to get more rest and better to proceed on another day.

Rick was relieved because one or two of the questions had touched a nerve and especially when he was asked about his drug use and he was pleased when the officers had left.

After they had departed the doctor also confirmed they had determined that Rick had heroin in his bloodstream when he was admitted and that he wished to know how bad his habit was and how much he had been taking but Rick had no idea what amounts the brothers had been injecting into him but he was sure it was quite big amounts.

The doctor said he could perhaps be able to get Rick a prescription for methadone but that would need to be arranged in the morning to which Rick thanked him for his assistance but in his mind he doubted very much he would still be here by then.

He grabbed himself as much sleep as he could in the coming hours but once early hours came he slipped out of his bed and built his pillows up under the covers to give the impression the bed was still being slept in and proceeded to the toilet to change into his clothes.

He was very unsteady on his feet as he searched for the nearest exit and he knew that in all honesty he really needed a three or four day stay in the hospital but no way could he do that under the present circumstances.

He inched his way down the fire escape he had come across at the end of the landing and found himself out on the car park. He wished, at this moment, that he had a car waiting but it wasn't the case and he staggered and reeled to the first exit to the main road with intention of flagging down a taxi but it was now 5am and he would need to wait a while.

When he finally got in one the driver asked "are you sure you are ok mister? You don't look to good"! But Rick assured him he was ok and gave directions to his home address.

He still had some insane belief that Sarita would be there but he was shocked to see the extensive damage to her room and it was with a heavy heart he made his way to his own room and soon discovered that too was in a state of disarray and which ever things had not been broken had been stolen. They had done a thorough job without a doubt but Rick could see the air vent was still intact and had not been disturbed so he undid the screws until he had access and placed his hand inside to retrieve the money he had concealed.

It wasn't a great amount by now and he would certainly need to find another source of income!

By now he was very tired by the exercise he had put himself through and so he lay on the bed to get a little rest but fell into a deep sleep that he certainly must have needed and never woke until early afternoon the following day.

Once he woke he set about putting some semblance of order back into his room under the belief he was still the tenant.

The neighbour who lived below must have notified the landlord of the noise from above and he showed up in a blind rage demanding to know what Rick thought he was doing. He soon made it clear that Rick had to gather his belongings and give him his keys and vacate the premises. He rambled on about his religion and the shame and ranted mainly in his own language but the name Sarita could clearly be heard in his rants and Rick assumed it would serve no purpose trying to reason with him.

He gathered his belongings as quickly as he could fearing the landlord may contact Sarita's father or brothers!

He threw his worldly possessions into the back of the van and drove away rather angrily at events that had just taken place.

He was hurting and in a murderous mood and he cursed religion and especially cursed cursed muslims and his imagination ran riot with the promise to himself that should there be another victim he wished it to be muslim.

But for now there were more pressing matters. He was beginning to ache and crave a fix. Only an addict would know the feeling. It's an impossible urge to banish from your mind set and the only thought process that comes to the fore is the finding of what is needed to quell and satisfy that desire.

Once Rick obtained his supply he got into the

back of his van and smoked a little of his wares and promised himself that he would prefer to lose the use of the needle and even reduce the amount he smoked 'chasing the dragon'!

He felt the warm glow as he inhaled then curled up in a ball to get a little more sleep. He had decided that he may have to live in the back of the van because accommodation would be hard to secure now due to recent events and in particular this neighbourhood.

He knew he would no longer be even welcome to clean out the wheelie bins so he intended to sell the jet wash at the earliest opportunity, but not before he had thoroughly cleansed the interior of his living quarters.

He then purchased a thick foamed underlay carpet, sleeping bag and blankets and made a sort of curtain rail for his few remaining clothes. He also insulated the sides of the van and once he was completely satisfied that it would be worthy enough to live in he sold the jet wash to make his living space more roomier. He figured he no longer had a job anyway and so the jet was surplus to requirement.

Something else may come up thought because the world revolved around mobile businesses, mobile hairdressers, mobile nails….. Rick could go on and on and on he laughed inwardly to himself that maybe he could become a mobile murderer.

He tried to put the thoughts of killing to the back of his mind but it would prove to be an impossible task because his anger towards any member of the muslim religion would just consume his thoughts.

Of course he would prefer it to be the father, one of the brothers, the landlord or the nosey neighbour but that would be too indicative of his involvement and as angry as he was he wasn't rash enough in his judgement to find himself under arrest. No! He would select a random muslim when the time was ready.

He drove to the secluded spot where the coins were secreted inside the knot hole of the tree and the very instant his hand made contact with the bundle the intense erection once again put in an appearance.

He knew it would only be a matter of time before he was active again now he had them in his possession!

Meanwhile sixty miles away in Rochdale where Sarita had been sent to stay with one of her numerous aunties, she had pined for Rick endlessly and thought of him every moment of every day until the moment she had been presented with the video footage of Rick injecting.

It had tarnished her image of him completely and she felt repulsed as she watched it over and over. There was no doubting it was him and she felt betrayed and a little foolish that she hadn't spotted the signs herself.

In time she learnt to forgive her father and brothers and even reached the stage that she even thanked them for their assistance in ending the relationship.

She resumed her studies and never even considered wanting to contact Rick Or rekindle their romance.

She promised herself never to be so trusting with any man again.

Rick still held Sarita in very high esteem and would have placed her on a pedestal and for that reason he had already ruled out killing female muslims because he doubted he could do it. He thought an image of Sarita would be there should he have a female sacrificial altar.

He would search about and try to meet a nasty minded one who, in his opinion, deserved to die.

His whole world was now upside down again and someone would need to pay for his suffering.

He felt his life was a little worthless again and he needed to re-gather and save what little he could.

He knew the heroin must stop but for now all he could do was slowly reduce his intake on a day to day basis but he was determined to conquer this one demon. Obviously he had other demons but this was certainly the one that required his immediate attention.

He was no good to anyone whilst he was an addict and especially himself and in his mind he was always of the opinion that he and Sarita would one day soon meet again.

He was not to know of Saritas present situation and views because if he had known there was no doubting he would probably kill someone within the next hour he would be that incensed.

He prepared to spend his first night inside his van but was very restless as he recalled almost everything that had already happened since that first day he was released from prison.

It had been a runaway train from the word go but there was one thing that concerned him more than any other!

There was no sign of it stopping!

Chapter Nineteen

Rick considered moving to live in the neighbouring town of Batley but there had been a few racial attacks there and tensions were running high and so for the time being he decided to stay where he was and just take things day by day.

He had great difficulty coming to terms with what his town had become because it had become hugely over populated with immigrants and especially muslims and many of them with extremist views.

He wasn't racist and never had been but it had now reached the stage where nobody could even voice one concern for fear of being branded racist and he supposed most people adopted the same stance and preferred to remain silent.

The goal posts had moved slightly now and Rick had more than a little dislike towards them due to the brutality he had to experience from Sarita's family. He wasn't about to forget that overnight and he had every intention of making some muslim victim pay the ultimate price as he rolled a gold coin through his fingers and once again felt the urge and desire to kill.

He set about killing two birds with one stone because he would need to go deep into the local muslim area where he had lived until recently, in search of one of the many heroin dealers and would take this visit as an opportunity to find himself an unsuspecting victim and lure him into his eager clutches.

He approached one or two of the men by the phone box who just seemed to be sat about for no other reason than to do trade because they certainly weren't waiting to use the kiosk. He was met with suspicion by both of the men because having never dealt with him before there was a possibility he could be an undercover officer.

It seemed a stalemate until one rather shabbily dressed asian man declared that he had in fact sold Rick heroin before as he made his way into the kiosk to make a call. Rick remembered his face in an instant as being the one who traded with him when the brothers had held him captive in the van.

An exchange was now done with the other dealers ad Rick waited for the man to leave the phone booth to thank him and he also realised this man must be close to the brothers for them to have called him that night.

He decided in that instant that this would be his next target and that maybe he would need to follow him at a distance and await his movements but fortune was on Rick's side because the man squeezed his mobile phone contact number into Rick's hand and told him he was happy to accept him as a customer and also announced that he even delivered on occasions if the customer had difficulties reaching him.

"Manna from heaven" Rick thought and it was as if the man was offering himself on a plate to be a victim, Rick thanked him gratefully and promised him he would be in touch on a regular basis.

They both exchanged handshakes and both departed elated in their own way, the dealer believing he had ensnared another victim BUT Rick knowing their would only be one victim in any future proceedings that took place.

He walked away with a big smile on his face and he was fortunate in a way that the dealer wasn't aware of any recent altercations between himself and the brothers.

That turned out to be more than a blessing because as Rick walked the short distance back to where he had parked his van a car with blacked out windows pulled up alongside him and to his horror he realised Saritas brothers were the occupants.

One of which waved a gun and made it clear in no uncertain terms that Rick should leave this neighbourhood and never be seen in it again.

He attempted to talk but the worlds would not come out and as he stood there frozen to the spot he assumed they must have seen this as some sort of stubborn stace.

Rick's mind switched back on once he had

seen the safety catch released on the gun and
he set off running and he managed to get to
the safety of one of the narrow aisles that
lead you into the rabbit warrens and a
neighbouring street.
He had heard footsteps running after him
originally but they had now fell silent and
he knew they mustn't have felt comfortable
running about with a gun in the streets in
broad daylight .

Rick ran into the corner shop a little out
of breath and it seemed the coast was clear
he left and made his way to his transport but
not before asking the shop owner to forget
what he had just said because he had over
reacted and read the situation wrong due to
him being paranoid.
The shopkeeper assured Rick that he would say
nothing but picked the telephone up
immediately and rang the police station.

Rick wasn't to know but the shop owner had
been robbed on a few occasions at gunpoint and
was determined to rid the area of wannabee
gangsters around the area.

The police would arrive, take a statement and
be very interested in the chain of events and
report the matter back to a senior officer
which in this instance turned out to be James
O'Dowd.
Rick knew the two brothers were very dangerous
individuals and it was one of them he would

prefer to kill but he also knew it highly
unlikely that could happen because it would
point straight back to him.
He had settled for the next best thing!
The men at the phonebox because he seemed to
have some sort of connection with the brothers
and if he could even repay them back a little
of the pain they had put him through then he
would be satisfied..

     He thought it wise that he should stay out
of the area completely now because he was sure
they would eventually carry out their threat
and shoot him and it wasn't a risk he cared
to take.
It crossed his mind to arm himself and
purchase a gun but he dismissed the idea
almost immediately because he knew he could
always conceal his egg up his rectum but he
didn't really wish to have any sort of
difficulty that would come with the need to
conceal a gun each day.

     He retreated to the safe confines of the
van and stroked the gold coin in the one hand
and caressed the slip of paper with the
dealer's number and again became very hard
contemplating a method to use for the kill!

     He would need to guide the man in slowly
but surely , but the very first thing on the
agenda would be to build up trust and gain the
man's confidence.
He met him on a few occasions and bought larger
amounts each time although at this stage he

had practically weaned himself off of it altogether.

He knew that should he order smaller amounts the dealer may not deem it worth his while to go out of his way to deliver. He had built up a very good rapport with him by this time after several meetings and he was a user himself and on one occasion he had got into the back of rick's van to conduct the business and rick was overjoyed to witness that the man injected and as some addicts will tell you the process can sometimes be done a little easier by a companion doing the injecting and the man had let rick do the honours. There would be no need for any rushed activities now.

The snare was set! The rabbit would soon be in the headlights but by then it would be much too late, they would always wave each other off fondly when they parted and the man had no reason to suspect rick was anything but a good friend.

Rick's problem was he was needing to be seen injecting himself and the last thing he wanted was for his addiction to take a grip of him again so he wanted the killing to be sooner rather than later.

Each time he had planned around that day being the day something would occur to spoil the plans. The dealer would be in some rush to deliver to another customer and it seemed the opportunity would never come about but he knew that he needed to be patient.

He had already purchased the rat poison and mixed it into one of the sachets of heroin he had bought and set that package aside for the very special evening he had eagerly looked forward to.

He thought it was a fitting way to end his life anyway because he despised heroin and its dealers and he regarded them as no more than rats.

So it would be a very apt way for him to leave this planet, he had thought of disposing his body in a sewers and also had plans to burn him and his body but he knew he would do neither of those, as that would take all of the fun out of the proceedings and he would want to be disposing of this corpse in the middle of the muslim community and also in a very prominent spot.

It would be a little bit of revenge for the way they had treated him.

The hour couldn't come quick enough for Rick and all his preparations and plans be able to reach fruition.

The man showed up to meet Rick one evening and in a very agitated state because he had recently been arguing with one of his wives and when Rick sort of suggested they smoke a pipe of peace together and just relax the man needed no further encouragement as they both got into the back of the van.

They both just smoked a little weed first

and got a little stoned until things progressed to the heating of the contents of a spoon, Rick just let the proceedings take their course until he was sure the time was right for him to suggest to the man to relax and he would 'fix him up'.

He asked the man to hold and tighten his own tourniquet and after filling the needle with the contents of the 'special wrap' he injected it fully into the man's arm and sat back and waiting for his body to go into violent spasms and his head recoiled in shock with his eyes bulging trying to understand what was happening.

His old cellmate was that obsessed with the bulging eye process during a killing then how he wished he could be here to witness this as the man's eyes were virtually bursting out of their sockets.

He could not understand why Rick was stood over him calling him abusive names and he was completely in shock right until the very last throes of life remained in his body.

It would not take much longer before his body went limp and his lips had turned a nasty shade of blue. Rick decided that it was a harsh way to die and he could never wish to die in that manner after he gave the body an occasional kick to confirm it was lifeless.

Rick didn't feel confident enough to drive yet because of the drugs he had consumed, he didn't fancy the idea of sleeping in the back with the corpse and so he took a few blankets to the cab of the van and decided to sleep in there until the early hours of the morning and dispose of the body then.

He knew the layout of the area due to all of the bins he had once cleaned and he had already concluded that the best spot to dump 'a rat' would be in that area.

The bin area would be out of sight but the body would soon be discovered because of the continual use of them.

He had one final job that he needed to do and placed the obligatory gold coin into his hand and said a quick prayer for him but then Rick did a strange act and he couldn't understand why he had done this impulsive act but he carved a sign of the cross into the man's head.

This one deed would open up a hornets nest amongst the locals and would lead to heightened racial tension and riots such as the police had never witnessed before.

He drove to the area he had chosen and after picking his moment carefully simply dumped the body as if it was a black bin liner full of refuse.

The following morning would bring about havoc upon discovery of the body.

Chapter Twenty

In Rochdale Sarita woke up to the news that
her uncle had been found dead in a bin area
in Dewsbury.

The room was full of tears as her aunts
all wailed in unison like a bunch of banshee.
It did not matter they did not see each other
very often because they were still a close
family and she had lots of fond memories of
her favourite uncle.

It would be a traditional islamic funeral
and plans were put in place for Saritas
immediate family to travel over to be with
other family members in Dewsbury.
Upon arrival whole areas surrounding the
neighbourhood were ablaze with overturned

cars and unruly mobs roamed the streets in an aggressive manner as rumours abounded of it being a racial attack because of the sign of the cross etched into the man's forehead.

The memory was also still fresh in the mind of the baying mob of the recent slaying of the taxi driver as they descended on the police station with the crowd growing by the minute.

Many white people marched alongside of the mob and mingled with them to show their solidarity and although it was an uncomfortable alliance Rick just tagged along out of curiosity more than anything.

The police station was under siege and the superintendent demanded to be kept informed at every turn and demanded that O Dowd and Albrighton attend his office immediately.
"We need to go fucking public on this" he roared at them because it was now known to all , yet again, that the discovery of another gold coin.

The mob outside were capable of anything in this mood and would take a lot of appeasing. This was now the third murder with the coin being involved and the general public would need alerting and especially the mob outside to advert a race war.
O'Dowd was instructed that he should call an immediate press conference and only relay the necessary information and keep it to a minimum

and then that he himself would accompany him to address the ever increasing thing outside of the station.

Once some news leaked out to the crowd Rick smirked to himself knowing that he had now forced them to show their hand and he waited patiently for the speech that had been promised.

He watched carefully and studied the men delivering the speech from the raised platform and quickly gathered it appeared to be this O Dowd in charge of the investigation and he could see the stress etched alongside his face and just watching him under the cover of this vast crows made him feel comfortable and in control.

The police didn't seem to be making much headway at all and were at a loss to even explain the simplest of questions to the crowd.

Rick had a feeling of superiority and as for as he was concerned things had reached another level and he even gooded a few people stood alongside him to jeer and boo the police for all of their shortcomings.

He felt that he held all of the aces although he knew the efforts to detain him would now increase very substantially and he would need to be very careful from hereon in.

The crowd seemed a little appeased by the explanations they were being given although a few questioned why only one victim had been scarred by a sign of the cross.

The police superintendent decided that more
than enough information had been relayed and
called proceedings to an end but assured the
crowd that should there be any further
developments he would inform them at the first
opportunity.

    With this he spun on his heel and walked
back towards the station whilst whispering to
O'Dowd "I want this bastard in handcuffs! Do
you fucking hear me?"
O'Dowd couldn't wait to get away from him and
it would serve no purpose to even reply to his
previous comments.
"Let him go back to his office and leave us
to do the police work and we might make some
headway" O'Dowd thought to himself.

    Rick, meanwhile, walked away knowing he
had now poked the wasps nest and he would need
to stay very vigilant but something about
staring at the worried frown on O'Dowd's face
had given him an urge to taunt him further,
but he decided to shelve that idea until a
later date.
He felt a little uneasy walking through the
estate where he had dumped the muslim's body
but he returned to the scene of the crime like
a homing pigeon returning to it's coop but
made sure he also had the anonymity of being
lost among the crowd who were still angrily

gathered on many of the streets.

The press were having a field day on this one and had even given the killer the tag "The Mexican Murderer" because of the link to the coins.

Appeals were put in place requesting any information at all choose how irrelevant or insignificant it seemed to be reported and warning to be extra vigilant regarding their own safety and whenever possible only travel when they're accompanied by someone.

Rick found all of this rather amusing because surely they didn't think he was likely to be as rash as to commit another murder whilst there was all of this police activity.

There would be plenty of time for that BUT only when he was ready.

He was in charge of all of this not the police. He would pick his own date and victim when he chose to do so and he would be happy to go about his everyday life quite normally and never arouse suspicion and just play the waiting game.

How long that would be was anyones guess though because as he passed the bin area where the body had been placed he once again got an almighty erection and that would always coincide with the urge to kill.

He would need to restrain his demons and the split personality he had become, with this in mind he contacted his doctors surgery and

made an appointment , he was prescribed
tranquilisers after he had given the doctor
a few 'shrouded details' of his latest mood
swings.
The beast within him needed shackling for a
while and Rick knew this and very wisely took
the decision to leave the locality for a few
days and wean himself off of the heroin and
just stay out of the headlights of the police
investigation that was now very much in place.

He didn't need to go too far away because he
would still need to keep himself abreast of
any further reports and developments. He
recalled doing his map reading as a teenager
for his Duke of Edinburgh award on the
Yorkshire Moors just the other side of
Holmfirth close to Huddersfield and it
wouldn't be usual for any van to be parked for
long periods in this location because it was
one of the many local tourist attractions.
    During the day he would take long walks
across the moors and admire the views and have
the occasional pint at any of the public
houses he came across and nothing was out of
the ordinary to any of the unsuspecting
landlords and he quite easily blended in with
all of the other tourists and hikers.
    None of them would have the slightest idea
they had a mobile murderer in their midst!
Upon returning to the van each night he would
listen to all of the headlines on the local

news stations on the radio and go to sleep comfortably in the knowledge they were no nearer to solving none of the murders than when they had first began.

He became a regular figure trampling about over the next few days with many becoming familiar with his face and exchanging pleasantries and a little normality returned to his life.

He intended to stay a little longer than he did but for the fact one of his walks took him a little further than he intended and he found himself on Saddleworth Moors, he knew of the history of the place due to the infamous Ian Brady and the Myra Hindley, and the children that had been killed and buried here and knowing that some still remained buried gave him a very eerie feeling and he fell a few times over the wild heathers that grew, in his haste to leave the area.

He sat on a milestone to catch his breath and he felt very unnerved because although he was a killer himself and had taken the lives of innocent people he did not see himself in the same light as these monsters.

He felt very uncomfortable within himself and a guilty conscience nagged at him for the rest of the day and he cursed the day he had ever shared a cell with John Davidson who he felt was to blame for his actions. He was the man who had first put these thoughts into his head with his maniacal ramblings in the cell every evening.

Things had escalated for Rick very quickly since his release and he was that full of anger that he doubted he could stop these acts now even if he tried. He had become addicted to the sadistic pleasure that consumed him after each kill and now that the beast in him had been unshackled there was no going back!

He needed to leave this area without a doubt and all of the chilling coldness that the moor represented and he fet a little hypocritical saying a prayer for the deceased children but he did so anyway and left with a very heavy heart.

He drove through huddersfield and stopped in a small cotton town called Mirfield, on the outskirts of Dewsbury, for some lunch and to catch up on any of the local gossip.

The murders were still the topic of conversation on everyone's lips it seemed and upon picking up a local newspaper it shocked him to see a photograph of one of the coins staring up at him and appealing for any information as to if anyone had come into contact with anyone possessing such coins but Rick felt safe knowing that not even his ex partner Julie had actually laid eyes on the coins so it was likely to prove just a stab in the dark for the police!

They were clutching at strings!

He put the paper into his pocket and threw it

into the back of the van and he would study it more in depth a little more when he had more time on his hands.

It was possible to feel the tenseness in the town when he arrived in dewsbury and it transpired the deceased muslims funeral would be taking place in the coming days and Rick decided he would like to witness as much of that as possibly could to gain a little sick satisfaction as an added bonus to the actual murder itself.

It was difficult to see if the community relations had improved any on the day of the funeral because although many people had lined the streets muslims prefer their funerals to be very private and with only the male mourners being in attendance and although Rick managed to observe a little of the proceedings from a very discreet distance he and others who would wish to pay their respects would not be welcomed at the actual burial ceremony.

Not that he cared!

One less drug dealing scum was his opinion of the man and he felt the man thoroughly deserved what he had coming to him.

It wasn't until he paid close attention to some of the mourners that he realised that a few of them were known to him and he recoiled in horror when he recognised the father and the two brothers of Sarita in close attendance to the coffin and the reality quickly set in that it was a family occasion when he looked in the background at the women wailing and his heart skipped a beat when he spotted the girl who had totalluy stole ihs heart.

He was breathless admiring her beauty from a distance and he stared and stared not wanting to lose even one second of this moment and hoped against hope that her eyes would meet his but they never did.

His mind raced at the prospect of Sarita being back in the area and the possibility of him making some form of contact with her.

How would that be possible?

Would she even want to rekindle any of their relationship?

His heart began to slump even more now when the enormity of his actions had sank in, that she would now no longer want to ever speak to him again and who could blame her.

He had just killed one of her family members!!!

Chapter Twenty One

Rick was far too busy trying to catch Saritas attention to notice that the mourning crowd was interspersed with plain clothed police officers but fortunately he had not done anything that would draw attention to himself.

He sauntered away frying to work out a way of approaching the house and he quickly realised there was a queue of people at the door and down the pathway bearing flowers to give to the family and he raced to the local garage around the corner , after purchasing some he stood in the ever increasing queue himself.

He quickly scribbled his mobile number onto a scrap of paper and once he was greeted at the door he informed the recipient of the flowers to offer his deepest condolences to Satita for her loss , the lady in question summoned Sarita to the door and left her to speak to Rick.

A very tearful Sarita was shocked to see Rick but in her own way was also half pleased to see what she once regarded as a familiar and friendly face but she was also cautious in her approach and warned him of the reaction of the family if he should be seen here.

Other people were in attendance who could eavesdrop on their conversation so he quickly squeezed then scrap paper into her hand and implored her to call him.

That was the first bodily contact he had, had with her in what seemed an eternity and it felt so good to Rick and raised his spirits even for that one fleeting moment.

To the very experienced and observant O Dowd who watched everyone in attendance from a safe distance Rick looked to him no more than just a regular mourner offering his condolences.

After the visit at the hospital as well it was seeming that Rick was certainly having a lot of good luck on his side and he was fortunate to not have triggered any alarm bells by now.

The rest of the day passed without any incident and Rick found himself just sitting there staring at his phone hour after hour waiting for the expected call , which never came and he settled down for the evening feeling a little bit dejected that she had chose to ignore him.

Meanwhile Sarita lay awake and had picked her phone up on numerous occasions but she did not have the courage to call or text him because she was unsure what she would want to say so she put the matter on hold , anyway her family members needed comforting right now. She finally dropped off to sleep convincing herself that it was late and Rick would in no doubt be in some drug den somewhere.

She was still angry at the way in which she was betrayed by his actions and she certainly was not in a forgiving mood. Curiosity would get the better of her the following morning as she took a walk alone for the first time since arriving back from Rochdale.

She simply wanted Rick to explain his behaviour but if she was honest with herself she also wanted to hear his voice one more time. Even if it maybe the last time!

Rick had a very long standing habit of not answering withheld or private numbers but he knew in his heart that this one could be worth the risk and he went weak at the knees and needed to sit when he heard her voice at the other end of the line even though she did sound very cold towards him.

There was a little small talk concerning the recent funeral before Sarita confronted him with his heroin abuse and the video footage she had seen of him injecting.

She laughed hysterically once Rick had relayed all of the story to her of exactly what had occurred and she described it as utter bollocks and so far fetched and she demanded to know if he'd thought she was a complete fool.

He begged her to listen and on a few occasions some things did seem to make a little sense to her, more so once Rick had given her a complete detailed description of her father who he had never previously met. She was quite alarmed by some of Rick's revelations and told him she needed time to think and consider everything she had just been told, Rick begged her not to hang up and asked for her phone number with which she was not prepared to do.

Sarita felt under enormous pressure if what she had just heard was to be true and needed a few hours to herself to process all of this information.

She promised him she would be in touch and he had no reason to doubt her, he also had a lot to run through in his own mind.

He re-ran every moment of his spell in captivity by the brothers through his mind albeit with a much clearer head this time and it all came flooding back to him of the time they let him get out of the van to purchase the heroin and then inject himself.

Now he had a clear picture that this was more than likely the footage Sarita had been shown to portray him in a dark light.
Of this he had no doubts!

It also came to him in a flash that the one who conducted the sale was the very same one who had just been buried which made him less remorseful than how he had felt earlier.

In Fact he was now feeling elated that he had killed him and especially in the manner in which he had done so.

He walked around the rest of the day with his mind in a blur, but that minimal contact from Sarita had answered a lot of the questions that had been puzzling him.

Sarita was not quite ready to confront her brothers with what she had just been told and she was terrified to question her father, she also realised that should it be true she'd make her family aware that would put Rick's safety into jeopardy.

She was unsure how to approach it all and decided she wished to speak to Rick at greater length just to confirm exactly what she already feared.

Rick was eager to accept her invite when it came and they arranged to meet at a secluded spot in Dewsbury Park which they could both reach at short notice once the opportunity presented itself.

They didn't exactly throw their arms around each other in the manner they once did but the conversation flowed freely enough and Sarita presented Rick with the footage and informed him this was the one bit of evidence she was having difficulty coming to terms with until Rick explained the brothers were close by in the van and watching his every move.

To confirm his reasoning Rick requested she take a closer look at the man actually selling him the drugs because upto this point he had obviously been a faceless figure to her as she had only been interested in Rick's movements. "Oh My God! It's my uncle!!" she exclaimed and was completely taken aback. Everything was becoming so clear and apparent to her now, it was as if she had woken from a very bad dream.

She wanted to scream and shout at her brothers but knew she would need to bite her lip and stay composed.

Rick assured her he was prepared to go to any centre at all with her now where it was possible to take a drug test to confirm to her that he no longer had heroin in his bloodstream and if she wished he could also take her to the local hospital to confirm his injuries and how he had been dumped on the car park.

She had no wish to do so and felt very bad about how she had doubted Rick but she couldn't believe anything but the evidence she had been presented with. They were both filled with anger but for some strange reason they were both still a little strained with each other and they both sort of accepted that even if a relationship still could possibly exist it would certainly need a lot of work on it.

She was still not sure enough to give him

her number because he could always answer her calls at his leisure, but her situation was entirely different and she could be say in the wrong company should her phone ring so she felt for now that one way contact was the safest option for them both.

Even Though they felt a little more comfortable about each other now they had been faced with the truth it mattered little from a romantic point of view as they both just kissed on the cheek in a very platonic way when they parted company.

Rick had already accepted that the road ahead was likely to be a tricky one but it was a road he was prepared to travel because he loved this girl and she had been the only one who had been capable of taming this beast within him and just that period of weeks spent in her company had been worth years of any time with any other woman.

He knew that he must not put pressure on her and any decisions taken would be much better being taken by her, he would need to wait patiently but i'm sure that both of them knew that the only logical solution would be for them to run away together sooner rather than later because she would shortly be returning to Rochdale and he feared he may lose her again.

He wanted to see her every minute of every waking day but he knew that would not be possible considering the present circumstances. Sarita had shrugged the brotherly arm off that had just been placed around her shoulders and walk away rather than force any confrontation as it would serve no purpose at this moment in time.

She knew the situation would need to be considered very carefully and although she wanted to chastise everyone involved she knew that the likelihood of that happening would be by way of a written correspondence if she was ever well away from these domineering people.

"I cannot blame him" Sarita thought after all he had just been put through. She obviously knew he was still interested for him to make contact the way that he did.

"How could I ever make it up to him?" she thought.

It wasn't exactly her who had brutalised him but it may as well have been for placing him in the romantic tryst that she had.

Sarita was still a little standoffish and abrupt when her brother spoke to her and as he entered the room she left it and both the brothers quickly came to the conclusion that something was amiss. She could not contain herself any longer and said "Guess who I bumped into on Dewsbury Park?" And went onto relay "What an amazing story he had to tell me too…"

"Well, is anyone going to deny it?" She raged at the pair of them. It became obvious to

Sarita that it had all actually been true and had taken place. All of the shouted had attracted the attention of her father who entered the room , closing the door behind him so just the four of them remained.

Her father immediately slapped Sarita firmly across the face declaring her to be a bitch in no uncertain terms, she screamed as loud as she could but it would be futile because nobody would dare enter and involve themselves in what they considered to be "male issues".

The father was furious and snatched the phone from her hand as she attempted to use it and once again he slapped her much more violently that resulted in her landing in a heap on the floor sobbing uncontrollably.

She cursed herself for being a fool because now all escape routes now would be quickly closed and she doubted she would even see daylight again for months if not years. She attempted to reach for the phone but her father stamped on her arm to prevent her from reaching it, he reached down and scooped the phone up off the floor and threw it to the eldest brother and demanded he "Find this bastard!"

The log history of the phone didn't amount to much and so it soon became apparent which one was Rick's number and now they just needed to work out a way to flush him out which shouldn't be too hard.

The father beat Sarita mercilessly while all the time ranting about the shame brought on the family, she revealed things she hadn't intended to during the beating but she would have said or done anything to make it stop. She hoped she hadn't disclosed too much before she had passed out due to the pain.

Saritas aunt loved her dearly and when she saw the extent of her injuries she was concerned that she would have more to come so she suggested that it would be better to take her back over the border to Lancashire and away from "the boy" situation.

She knew that she had to word it in a way that made the father feel as if he was still in command of the situation and thankfully he readily agreed for Sarita to be moved out of the house and into the waiting car.

The brothers knew by now the very meeting place of Sarita and Rick and it was quite simple to send Rick a text saying "Can't speak, in company meet in the same place in an hour?"

Rick received the message and was a little disappointed that it wasn't accompanied by at least one kiss but he accepted it was early days and they would need to build each other's trust up once more.

"On the plus side, at least she wants to meet me again" he sighed, he loved feasting his eyes on her at every possible chance anyway so he hurriedly prepared himself for this 'date'.

The brothers made a few calls and picked up a few friends enroute to the park to ensure that all directions of escape were covered and it would be impossible for anyone to get away from what was about to take place.

Rick parked the van close to the entrance of the park and whistled and skipped his way through and around a small lake to the meeting place.

He was in a very happy frame of mind until he looked over his shoulder and realised a very stocky individual was following him and would guess he was about fifty or so yards behind him but even from that distance it was clear to see that the man was of a muslim appearance and he spent that much time looking over his shoulder that he failed to see another muslim come out of the bushes and swing a bat forcefully towards his face.

If anything he was thankful that the first blow was heavy enough to concuss him because what followed from all of them amounted to a very calculated and sustained beating that only ceased when witnesses to the assault came from around the corner out on an innocent stroll and must of wondered what they had just strolled into.

The middle aged couple helped Rick to his feet and sat him on one of the benches but when they said they were going to ring the police Rick pleased them to not call them, as it would only cause him more trouble.

He did not wish to stay in this spot alone for fear that they would return and finish him off, they would have certainly killed him had this lovely couple not stumbled upon matters. He asked them to support him if they could to one of the well lit exits and he would ring for one of his friends to pick him up and they said they would remain with him until someone came but he assured them that he was fine, he could see his van and he did not wish the couple to know it was his.

Once they had departed he rolled himself along the wall in a great deal of pain and what had first seemed to be a short distance took him a very long time to reach due to his injuries. He threw the door open accessing the back of the van, closed the door behind him and collapsed in a very pained state gasping and groaning until he fell asleep.
He hurt but at least he had survived the attack.

Chapter twenty two

The couple in the park were concerned for
Ricks safety and almost as soon as they had
left they notified the police about what they
had just witnessed but apologised that they
couldn't give a better description of any of
the assailants.

They gave directions as to where they
had left the victim and after leaving their
names and addresses they went about their
business.

A patrol car was despatched to the park
area and began to do a sweep of the park and
the surrounding vicinity in the hope of
finding the injured man.

Back at the station Graham Albrighton had
called a meeting in the absence of O'dowd and
attempted to assert his authority and make the
case his own.

The time had passed for office 'romance'
and he needed , he felt , to focus all of his
energy on the matter in hand and that was there
was a madman out there on the loose murdering
innocent people at will.

He instructed every available officer to
do yet another round of door to door inquiries
in the hope they found even the slightest

detail that they had missed on previous visits.

He got the control room to put out a call to all units to forget what they were doing right now and return to base to receive further orders.

Rick was groaning in pain in the back of the van and in a great deal of discomfort and he knew it would be unwise to attend the hospital after his previous stay. He would need to self treat his wounds in the coming days and wait for mother nature to do its own healing.

The patrol car meanwhile had circled back round and had begun to take an interest in the parked van and one of the officers had just got out of his car to have a closer inspection when his colleague shouted for him to leave it because they were required to report back to the station immediately.

Fortune favoured Rick yet again although he was unaware of just how close he had been to facing some very awkward questions.

He was certainly having more than his share of luck but then again so did Peter Sutcliffe, the Yorkshire ripper who had been questioned and released on several occasions by the very same West Yorkshire police force. Call it ineptitude or call it what you may but Rick had escaped the clutches of the law yet again and they would live to regret it in the coming months.

When Rick felt able enough to drive he got behind the wheel but winced in pain at each corner he needed to turn and it was clear to him that many of his ribs had been broken.

His only consolation was that during the beating he had picked up on snippets of conversation between his attackers and he knew that Sarita had not set him up.

They had screamed in his face about the text message and he knew that it was them who had sent it and his main concern was for her safety but how could he possibly be able to contact her now.

The previous time apart had been very difficult but he imagined this time round it would be virtually impossible to have any contact at all, she would be a virtual prisoner in her home for the foreseeable future.

At least she knew the truth now and the bad light he had been portrayed in was no longer in her thoughts.

Saritas aunt apologised for the lock on the bedroom door but she informed her that it was at her father's insistence and had she refused to do so then he may take his daughter back to his own home and the aunt stressed she was sure neither of them wished that to happen for her own safety.

She cried herself to sleep still nursing her injuries and completely unaware of the severe beating rick had taken, she was furious with her family for the way she had been treated and promised herself they would not be able to control her forever and the very first time they let their guard down she would flee and never return.

Her heart pined for Rick and she was appalled at the way her family had took it upon themselves to treat him so severely.

She went to sleep remembering the one promise they had both made to each other that should they ever find themselves apart they would meet on the cliff tops of Flamborough head and it gave her great comfort knowing that is what she intended to do once her aunt relaxed her restrictions a little.

Rick knew, by now, in his heart that if Sarita were able to contact him then she would do so and obviously not hearing from her would mean her family were once again placing limitations on her and he just had to hope that one of them wouldnt be to send her back over to her native country because love may be able to conquer all but that situation of being continents apart would be a very insurmountable position in Rick's opinion.

At this point he was very anti-muslim and wanted to strike the first one that he came across but he just as quickly dismissed the thought because he had met some very nice people within that very same community and he wasn't prepared to tarnish them all with the same brush.

However slight the hope was that he and Sarita would meet again he definitely needed to hold on to that thought as it would be the only thing that kept him in a positive frame of mind.

He crept further in and out of the neighbourhood and it soon became apparent that she no longer seemed to be within the family home.

He stared at each bedroom window hoping for the slightest sign that she may be in one of them but all to no avail and even as extreme as he now knew they could be he doubted they had imprisoned her in the very same room as he had been held.

"No father would do that to a daughter he thought" surely not"?

He cursed religion and all it brought with it.

He parked the van up for very long periods and instead chose to walk and make his body work again which was all part of the healing process and in no time whatsoever he felt completely able bodied again apart from this discolouring of the bruising around his face which didn't make him a pretty sight at all.

He was walking around one fine sunday morning and realised a full mass was taking place at the church of his christening as a small boy, Saint Paulinus and without hesitating found himself on one of the pews at the back of the congregation.

Apart from his visit to the confessional box on the previous occasion he had long since passed on religion and hadn't been a practicing christian for many years, he sat and half heartedly listened to all of the sanctimonious sermons as they were delivered. Father Hinchcliffe was aware of the new face in the gathering and was sure he had met him before but couldn,t quite place his face but was sure it would come to him.

Rick felt it would be wrong of him to go up and receive the holy communion bread at the altar because he wasn't here to be saved or blessed, he had come more out of curiousity than anything else.

He recalled being scared as a small child to commit any sin whatsoever and imagined all children having the same fears.

This was the hold the church would have in the eyes of a child. He recalled being awe struck and very fearful of the consequences and on reflection it made him very angry.

Father Hinchcliffe stared at him from the pulpit as he delivered that weeks sermon and there was something very unsettling about the man,

He certainly did not seem as if he had come to worship.

Rick laughed inwardly when the point of the sermon seemed to suggest that is was all about loving one's neighbour and indicated that we are all equal and no bias towards our fellow man should exist.

Before he knew it the offering tray was placed in front of him full of coins and notes which in his opinion people could ill afford anyway and it was yet another indication of the pressure people are placed under by the church to contribute each week.

He hit the bottom of the tray with his clenched fist and sent the tray and its contents scattering throughout the aisle of the church and before he could prevent himself began to shout " fuck the church" and exploded with rage as he screamed " religion ruins the world" and stormed out of the building to get away from these pious people.

All of the crowd gasped at the unexpected intrusion to their usually quiet service on a Sunday but the priest hushed the congregation and asked for forgiveness for the man.

It was the topic of conversation outside the church on conclusion of the service and the priest assured everyone that everything was fine and the man possibly just needed a little help and was encountering a few difficulties at this time in his life. Once the congregation had left though the priest sat down and reflected on the mornings events and went through old school photos of classes who had received their first communions at the church because he wished to put a name to the face who seemed such a troubled soul.

He wondered what could possibly be causing him such anguish and almost in the same instant he recalled the visitor to the confessional box who declared that he THOUGHT he may have killed someone but the priest dismissed it at the time because the man did not seem sure that he had actually killed someone.

He was also unsure that it was even the same man due to the bruised face of the individual this morning, maybe it was someone else who was just a little disturbed.

He picked the phone up with the intentions of ringing the police but this would also go against the priest vows and he was undecided as to what to do.

He decided eventually that maybe the man hadn't even killed anyone at all and it would be a betrayal of trust and at this moment in time if the man was doubting his own faith the last thing he as a priest, would wish to do is drive the man even further away from his religion.

He was torn for a few more minutes but finally placed the receiver back onto the cradle of the telephone and went about his usual sunday business.

Rick was certainly not aware of all of his recent good fortune but on this particular occasion it seemed that even his god and religion had saved him this time.

Rick spent the rest of his day visiting all of the places from his childhood. Saint

Paulinus school and Saint John Fishers school and just sat there and reflected on just what a controlling thing religion can be. Yes at this moment in time he resented the islamic faith but in all reality was his catholic upbringing any different?

He did not have many fond memories at all and remembered all of their names and faces like it was yesterday, nuns and priests all prepared to mete out corporal punishment like it were the most normal thing to do.

Small children with battered and bruised hands from continual canings or being struck with thick heavy set rulers about the head or legs if you were lucky.

They had a lot to answer for and Rick felt that the introduction to brutality at a tender age was far from conducive to a happy childhood and he doubted it would have been much different in other different religious teachings.

Chastisement was there order of the day back then, either at school or in the home and thankfully nowadays much of it is frowned upon but this mattered little to Rick in his angry and confused state.

This anger would need to be harnessed because if it wasn't then sometime soon some poor innocent soul would be facing the consequences.

Chapter Twenty Three

O'Dowd was very irate when he returned to his duties to discover that Albrighton had redirected all of his officers to do what he had required them to do instead and he was tempted to complain directly upstairs to their commanding officer but decided against it but not before they both had a very heated exchange.

He had only taken the one day off to attend a family funeral and he felt that on his return a lot of chaotic instructions had ensued and he had, had enough now of Albrighton attempting to undermine his authority. Incidents had been set aside to be investigated at a later date because they all seemed to be drug related. Albrighton stressed that at this moment in time the murder of innocent people would need to be made the priority and then to conclude the argument he very smugly informed O'Dowd that all of his decisions had been given the seal of approval after discussing matters with the superintendent.

Albrighton almost smiled in his face as he relayed this information and did everything except utter the word "CHECKMATE". O'Dowd absolutely despised the fact he needed to work alongside this individual and resented everything about him and especially his way of enforcing the law.

Throughout O'Dowd's career he knew that more often than not any investigation regarding any crime usually led to the solving of other unrelated crimes and he had made many arrests adopting this very same policy.

It would serve no purpose going up to see his superior because the decision had already been reached to put all other crimes on the back burner for now.

He did not wish to create an atmosphere around the rest of his colleagues so for the time being he reluctantly agreed it was the right course of action.

Once O'Dowd had the office to himself though he leafed through a lot of the paperwork that had been put to one side and there was certainly seeming to be a lot of drug related assaults to suggest maybe a turf war was taking place. He pursued detail after detail but all he had in front of him was a gang of unknown individuals had assaulted another unknown person and a few suspicions of a

parked white van which could belong to anyone
really because no one had even thought to take
the registration number, not like he had much
to go on but he always kept an open mind that
one crime always led to another and he pit all
of this paper work into his briefcase to study
at home.

It wasn't as if anyone else would be
wishing to look at them now they had been given
alternative directives by Albrighton. Lots of
divisions were appearing within the incident
room and O'Dowd knew this was likely to be
detrimental towards everyone working
together as a team.
O'Dowd had always believed that strength in
a team came about through unity and on this
occasion he was thankful that the public
domain were not aware of all of this
discontent because if they did not have the
support of the public then it was a lost cause.
They would wish to sleep soundly and safely
in their beds each night knowing that their
police force were dealing with this
professionally with the matters at hand.

O'Dowd accepted that some good may come
from revisiting homes that had been given a
knock previously but he also had a lot of
niggling doubts that they were somehow
missing something that was staring them in the
face.
Rick's mood the following morning had not
lessened any and just about everyone he came

into contact with he reacted grumpily and had no patience whatsoever.

He sat on a wall in a very reflective mood and in a world of his own until a friendly voice snapped him out of his self induced coma like state of mind. "How you doin Ricky? Long time no see" asked Dale Barnwell a long standing friend.

He would have known without enquiring, that Rick would have more than likely been in prison because he had been in there with him a few times down the years because Dale was somewhat of a repeat offender.

He sympathised with Rick upon hearing of the news of his ex partner decamping with the children and informed him he hadn't been having much of a good time himself.

Dale suggested that they both forgot the world and all of the problems it brought about and that the pair of them spent the day getting drunk and stoned.

Rick had known Dale for many years and they had even committed burglaries together in their youth. He thought Dale looked a little unkempt with his ungroomed stubble and with his slightly dark skinned appearance he could quite easily be mistaken for a muslim. They both spent the day having numerous beers and laughing at amusing incidents they both recalled concerning each other and Rick enjoyed the day because he had forgotten what it was like to laugh and smile although every

now and then he would look across at Dale in
his drunken like state in a very agitated
manner and Dale would need to calm him down
but never once knowing what was disturbing his
friend so much.

In the final public house of their hastily
arranged pub crawl they were asked to leave
by the landlord because he did not like the
way Rick was behaving and by now they were in
a completely different area on the outskirts
of Leeds and the proprietor decided he did
not wish to take the risk of Rick becoming
violent.
They both staggered along the road devouring
some Chinese food they had just bought and
Rick ate the food like a starving wolf and
began to realise he hadn't even eaten for the
three days previous.

They would need to catch a taxi back to
their home town because it was a journey of
six or seven miles and in their present state
they could not have walked six or seven yards
let alone miles.
They both got into the rear seat of the taxi
and the asian music station was quite annoying
to Rick. Dale watched him do something very
strange under the influence of the alcohol.
For Rick it was as if he was in a trance like
state and the music wasn't helping the
situation any.

Dale observed Rick reach down and begin
to take one of his laces from his shoe which

intrigued him for a little while and he
laughed at the unusual behaviour right up to
the point that Rick was about to place the lace
over the drivers head and Dale grabbed his arm
and stopped him in his tracks.

"For fuck sake! What the fuck was going
off there?" he thought.
Once they both got out of the cab there was
a polite silence but Dale was concerned at
leaving Rick in this state and frame of mind
while he limped along carrying one shoe in his
hand.
Although he seemed fine now Dale thought it
wise to get him off the streets and he laughed
to lighten the mood when Rick said he lived
in the back of a van but once he clambered in
with him he was surprised at just how homely
Rick had made it.

He sat and began to make a joint whilst
he watched Rick re-lace his shoe and put it
back onto his foot as if the recent events had
not taken place. Dale wasn't to know any
better and thought it was an isolated incident
so thought better of raising the matter.

He was still concerned about what he had
just witnessed and the conversation became
very limited as another joint was passed
around.
Rick had got out of the van to urinate and was
doing so up the side of the van. Dale in a
moment of boredom had picked up the newspaper
that was at the side of him and began to read

the headline out loud regarding the coins and
foolishly shouted and asked Rick "Hey didn't
you burgle some coins a while ago?"

Rick shouted back that he was just going to
get some cigarettes from the cab at the front
of the van and placed a large screwdriver in
the waistline of his jeans and made his way
to the inside again.
    The topic of conversation changed and
Rick could have left it at that thinking that
no more would come of it but he was not
prepared to take that chance and the next time
Dale had began to make a joint and had taken
his eyes away from Rick he had took out the
concealed weapon and in a flash he had struck
it through Dales throat so forcefully that the
end of the screwdriver had almost pierced the
side of the van and impaled him.
    He sat back in his original resting place
and watched excitedly as Dales throat and
mouth made a series of gurgling noises and his
body went into spasms . He moved in closer
because he now seen exactly what his cell mate
had described with the bulging eyes.
These were wide open in shock and disbelief
at what had just occurred and even when the
head slumped when he was finally lifeless he
kept lifting the head up again by the hair to
stare into those haunted eyes.
    This was the death that fascinated him
more than any other and he never slept for the

remainder of the night preferring instead to stare into the horror of the bulging pupils.

It was now daylight and he needed to dispose of the body. He did not want the corpse to remain in the van and panic began to settle in a little.

He had a thousand questions for himself, "How drunk had he been last night, would anyone remember the pair of them together, should he run the risk of giving him the coin as his parting gift from this world?"

He was still fascinated by the eyes and he became very excited when he looked down at the body. He tried to pretend in his mind that he hadn't actually killed a friend. Everyone so far had been relative strangers and he preferred it that way, because of his muslim appearance Rick painted a picture in his mind of it being one of his assailants rather than Dale.

He unzipped his fly and masturbated furiously in the corner of the van and when he finally ejaculated he walked over to Dale and forced his eyelids to close because the eerie stare was getting to him a little.

"You shouldn't have read the newspaper" Rick whispered into Dales ear as if to say that this was his own fault.

He set about cleansing the interior a little although there hadn't been too much blood due to the slender pointed stabbing of the screwdriver.

He still didn't wish to take too many risks though and stripped the carpet up and rolled Dale up inside of it, but not before he placed a gold coin into the palm of his hand and rather bizarrely wished him a safe journey.

This death left him a few guilty pangs due to their friendship but Rick thought what else could he have done in the circumstances. Dale had not seemed to have much positive going off in his life anyway so to condone his own behaviour a little Rick convinced himself that in a way it was perhaps a blessing for him rather than a prolonged life of sadness.

Rick wished it had been a muslim though all the same but it was too late for that now because the deed had been done.

The body count was beginning to stack up now and Rick wasn't to know it but his killing spree was far from over!

Chapter twenty four

Rick felt uncomfortable looking at the body and felt he may attract attention to himself by sitting in the front behind the wheel whilst not driving anywhere and so decided that even though it would be risky dumping it during the daylight hours that it was what he needed to do.

His problem was he prefered to dispose of it in a prominent spot where it would be easily found because he was enjoying the cat and mouse chase with the police.

He felt it served no purpose actually killing if the body was to be laid and undiscovered for weeks, months or even years because he was relishing his moment in the spotlight and each time a body was found it gave him a little of additional excitement and although it couldn't compare with the killing it still created an adrenalin rush within him.

He decided that a small tow path by some playing fields would be the ideal location and sat in his cab waiting for that one moment when a few dog walkers and joggers had passed and quickly as he could dragged the bundle to the rear and just rolled it out and placed it on the grass verge.

He looked all around and was confident he had not been seen and even if someone had from a distance it would just appear that he had dumped a roll of carpet.

He drove away at speed and now he just needed to sit back and wait for the proverbial shit to hit the fan, he turned in to all the local radio stations for the next day or so but nothing at all had been reported and he was staggered to think that hundreds of people by now had actually walked or jogged past the body without even taking the slightest notice of it.

He realised that he would soon need to sort out an additional source of income from somewhere because his funds were becoming quite limited so he went to the D.H.S.S and set about applying for his first payment since being discharged from prison but it soon became clear he was unlikely to receive anything due to him having no fixed abode and rick became very aggressive in his tone in his tone of responding to the officious civil servant and the whole office became aware of all the of the shouting taking place and summoned for the security guards.

When one of them had motioned to place a hand on Rick's shoulder he seen this has an affront and arched his head ready to headbutt the guard but thought better of it once he realised that a phone call to the police had just taken place so he raced out of the office and got lost in the crowd in the town centre.

The police officer who took the was accustomed to calls from the D.H.S.S because they would come through on a daily basis and he scribbled scant details down all the time yawning as he did so.

"We will get someone to you as soon as we can" he declared knowing that was unlikely to happen because reports had just come in of a few small children playing football who had discovered a body in the nearby playing fields.

O'david stared down at the corpse and instructed the officers who had been given the task of protecting the scene to give no indication of the coin found in the man's hand at this moment of time.

He stared at the screwdriver still imbedded in the victim's throat and was repulsed at the levels of violence the killer was prepared to use to carry out these heinous crimes.

He had been quiet for a while but he had certainly returned with a vengeance and O'david wondered how many of these scenes he would need to visit before the man was arrested which he hoped wasn't the case because no way would O'david be satisfied being in retirement if this man was still at large, he would have felt he had let the public down and himself, he was determined this man needed to be behind bars before he even contemplated placing slippers on his feet and lighting his pipe .

The police officer who had taken the call from the D.H.S.S had simply scribbled Rick's name down on a scrap of paper and upon terminating the call he just crumpled up the paper and threw it into the waiting waste paper basket which was his way of saying NO FURTHER ACTION, he was also quite angry to have been notified that all police leave had been cancelled for the foreseeable future, he wasn't looking forward to informing his partner that yet another foreign holiday would need to be shelved unless she would wish to go along with the children.

" a policeman's lot is not a happy lot " he thought to himself.

Upon investigation by the murder squad it transpired that dale bernwell was an habitual criminal who very few people would miss really, his family had long since washed their hands of him and he had burgled many of his neighbours and they would be hard pressed to find anyone who had a good word to say about him but the bottom line was he he was still someone's son and the parents would need notifying.

Question were asked as to who did the associate with and did anyone know his latest movements.

He had been out of his family circle for many years and it wasn't a particularly close friends with very few family friends photos and only snaps they could get of dale was when her was much younger, theydidnt feel it would be appropriate to use a prison or police photograph and so after being given the tearful mothers permission senior police officers gave the go ahead to release the photograph to the press and to run the story and also accompanying that was a £50.000 reward offered by a few local businessmen. With any information leading to the capture of the murderer the reward would be paid immediately.

The old adage about their being honour amongst thieves and criminals only exists to a certain degree and once a monetary carrot is dangled in front of them most would sell their own grandmothers.

Rick had never let the few of his friends who had shown the coin to have too close a look and the thing was they would never even contemplate Rick being a killer. Oh he had no doubt that if any of them had put two and two together he would have already been sold down the river but his close friends were always too stoned or wired to take much notice of what was going on in the real world anyway and were too busy with their own demons to worry about anyone else, most everyday events would go completely over their heads.

Yet another example of the continued good fortune Rick seemed to have been blessed with. Even the altercation at the D.H.S.S could have led to an awkward bout of questioning.

There was no doubting that these coins seemed to have been given some ancient holy blessing but how long could that good luck hold out?

Things were beginning to relax a little around sarita although she was still only permitted out in the garden for a few short periods and only then if she was accompanied by her aunt and/or other family members and she knew she would need to be very patient and wait her moment. If she attempted to flee now and it proved to be unsuccessful she knew the shackles would be firmly put in place and she may never even get another opportunity.

"No! Patience would be the key " she thought has she helped her aunt fold up all of the dry washing from the line.

Oh how she wished she could get even one message to rick, she didn't doubt that his love for her would be any less but how long could he be expected to wait for her.

She would need to purloin any money that she could come across in the house and even then only taking small amounts so as to not arouse suspicion. Her day would come when she could flee, she felt sure of that and when that time came she would certainly need readily available funds.

Had she chosen this particular moment in time to escape it would have been a fruitless journey to drewsbury to find rick because he had decided to move from the area because of the very large police presence who now seemed to be on every corner and knocking every door and stopping every vehicle coming in and out of the town.

Additional officers had been drafted in from all of the outlying forces and everyone's movements would be monitored for however long it took for the investigation to get a breakthrough on this case.

Rick knew that his only option had to be to move a good distance away after the one occasion when he had been pulled over for routine questioning and been shown a photograph of the deceased it had unnerved him a little.

He had been acting as calm and composed as he could and had not even realised until he had drove away that the kinder surprise egg containing the coins had sat and nestled comfortably upon his dashboard throughout the police questions.

At the first opportunity he could find a quiet place to park up he pulled over and got into the back and after lubricating his anal area he once again inserted the egg into his rectum, only this time promising himself it would never be taken out again except to do his toilet duties and then it would be replaced immediately after completion.

Rather than run any risk anyway it would seem a wise move to just leave all of this behind him and after filling the tank with fuel he set off towards the north coast and headed for Flamborough although he had not intended to! When he had originally set off he was just intending to go to the coast but it was as if he was drawn to the cliffs like a magnet.

He would prefer to burgle somewhere before he set off because now he had filled the tank he had barely any money at all, but only a fool would have considered doing burglaries in an area swamped with innumerable uniforms.

He didn't need anything to be too rewarding he wasn't looking for lots of high maintenance money. Just a bit of petty cash here and there would suffice.

With that in mind he recalled when he would never use the highways when he absconded from an approved school in case it attracted needless attention and he would always go down the railway tracks because not only did it keep him out of sight of prying eyes it also had the added bonus of a few of the more smaller stations always having ready cash available in the ticket office.

He presumed that was because the crime levels were quite low in these quiet little suburban villages and so they would trust to leave the money about and fully expect to have faith in it still being there in the morning.

Rick had run away from approved school on several occasions and each time he would follow the self same route and he would always be staggered to see that no lessons had been learnt from any previous burglary Not that he would complain as he stuffed his pockets with notes.

That had been many years before but he doubted anything had changed much except perhaps the denominations of the notes.

He had chosen to enter a small village station called micklethorpe just outside of leeds. He was glad he had picked this one because it was a wise choice because little had changed as he climbed through the broken window he had just broken in the early hours of the morning.

He made very little noise but he doubted it mattered the station was that secluded there would be no one to disturb within a hundred yards of the place.

He would have thought that by now in the present age they would have purchased a safe but to their loss they hadn't and as Rick shone the torch from his phone into the ancient wooden drawers by the ticket window there was a few stacks of five, ten and twenty pound notes which Rick gratefully swept up and considered leaving a thank you note but thought better of it!

He was happy with his evening's work as he counted up £ 380 in the back of the van , it wasn't exactly a king's ransom but it was

certainly more than enough to spend a week at the coast and he may even double back and look at another small train station to burgle on another evening.
He slept soundly and looked forward to his road trip in the morning.

Chapter Twenty Five

Julie hortson had endured quite a brutal life right from being a small child and things hadn't improved much throughout her adult life having had a succession of failed relationships and the most recent one ending with her having to be operated on for a broken eye socket at the main hospital in hull the place of her birth.

While she was small she always remembered

her parents fighting and arguing and swore her own life would not follow in the same path but unfortunately it had and if anything even on a worse scale.

Her only fond memories were as a child visiting flamborough for family holidays in a caravan and it wasn't like the squabbling between them would end at them times it just gave her a little respite because she could get lost in a world of her own while she walked along the cliff tops or along the beach.

This was the reason she was now setting of to return there and just get lost in the moment and sit on the cliff tops while she watched the waves crash in against the bottom of the cliff face.

Her relationship had been deteriorating for a long time and she should've left when he hit her the first time but she had preserved falsely believing that things would change. Hadn't even told friends of her own to never accept violence and always walk away and end the relationship. She felt foolish that she hadn't done the same as the advice she had offered.

She had been apart from her family for many years as with most families in similar circumstances she felt she had no one to turn to.

That was still the case now but while she had laid in her hospital bed each day and night she had promised herself faithfully that she would not be returning to the marital home. She was very thankful that there had been no children to consider because she was unable to conceive and that was probably down to the some of the beatings she had taken over the years.

There were far too many to pinpoint any particular one but one thing she did know for sure that this last one was the final straw and had almost killed her.

She was never at anytime prepared to report any of the incidents to the police and preferred to suffer in silence although this could prove difficult at time due to the constant visits from her partner begging forgiveness and promising faithfully it would never happen again.

His voice would go through her and half the time she wouldn't bother even taking the words in. not that it mattered because it was the self same words she had heard over and over. She gave him every indication that things were going to be fine and that they would work things out and she also readily agreed that yes a lot of it was her own fault and she had a lot to answer for.

"How dare you" she would think to herself but wouldn't have dared voice her opinion because the last thing she wanted was one of his outbursts and any disruption on the ward.

Some of the nurses said they could prevent him visiting but julie declined the offer.they would try to get her to discuss how her injuries had come about but she would prefer not doing so.

The nurses would not need informing, they had encountered many victims of domestic abuse and that most victims retreated into their shells.

Julie wanted him to be under the impression that all the damage had been repaired and they were 'the perfect couple' and she would soon be returning home, if she gave him any indication anything was amiss it would ruin all of her dreams and plans she had imagined whilst laying in this hospital bed and from the very moment she had been returned to the bed from the operating theatre.

When she had seen how unsightly she looked in the mirror in the bathroom she could of cried and no way was she ever going through this again.

He was under the impression she was in the hospital for another three days but the doctor had passed her as fit to be leaving the following day.

She sympathised with the torrent of abuse the hospital staff would have to endure once he discovered her absence but most of them were aware of her situation and would have probably wished her luck.

Julie was still in quite a bit of pain but she had been given strong painkillers on her discharge prescription and no words need to be spoken as she left and in actual fact the nurse seemed to sense the situation and took julie down a remote staircase that led to the fire exit and the outside world albeit in a very calm quiet part of the hospital grounds. The nurse gave her a quick hug, waved her off and wished her well for the future and returned to her duties.

This was julie's biggest adventure for many years but it was a journey that must be taken, she knew he would search everywhere throughout hull to find her and he had many more friends than her.she didn't really have any because that had been all part of his control pattern and he turned her into a very reclusive person afraid to speak to anyone for fear of incurring his jealous wrath.

She had decided to make herself a new life at one of the coastal towns on the north coast but before she put the plans into action she wanted to just sit on that cliff top and relive her childhood she wanted to start the day with a happy memory and that was then how she intended her life to remain.

Fate intended to deal her a cruel blow.

Mei ling had originally come to england on a tourist visa from china about one year before and had already overstayed but she didn't feel she had been given enough time to do what she wished to do which was learn the english language much better than what she did now, when she spoke it was very broken english and very difficult to understand.

She had been paying privately for lessons and working in one of her uncle's chinese restaurants to pay for it and he was prepared to hide her for as long as she wished to stay because she was his favourite niece and was eager to earn and all of the customers would compliment him on her efficient manner and politeness and she was certainly an asset as far as her uncle was concerned.

Should she return to china it would perhaps difficult to return again so easily and she felt her best method of learning would be to remain here even if it was illegally, it was a chance she was prepared to take and the only real concern she had was that she did not wish to bring any trouble to her uncle or his business.

When it was her days off she would travel from city to city with her camera and capture lots of famous landscapes, she was determined that even if she did have to go back to her motherland she would have lots of memories to take with her.

It was on their excursions that she would practice her english by speaking to as many strangers as possible, many would look at her in confusion and she would know instantly that she had pronounced something wrong again and especially if they laughed.

England always seemed a busy place to her and

people always rushing here and there in a helter skelter manner and they had little or time, it seemed, to even stand and talk to each other let alone a little chinese girl who couldn't string two words together and could be time consuming if they were to permit her. She had been fascinated by london when she first visited it but was very alarmed how chaotic public transport could and and especially on the underground tubes.

More often than not on these excursion that she would get lost, not only in london, it had happened on visits to all of the other major cities with major landscapes to photograph. Her uncle had warned her many times of the dangers of traveling alone but she paid no attention and always felt confident in her own ability to recognise any risky situation and thus far she had managed to avoid trouble.

The more time she returned safely they uncle had to agree with her that she had gained a very strong confidence about her and was maturing into a very worldly lady.

On this particular day she had caught a train from leeds to york or she had presumed it was the correct train but something did not seem right at the time and she got off at one of the smaller stations after perhaps half an hour into the journey.

She would need to return the route she had just come and so crossed over the small bridge and over to the other side of the station.

It was a quaint little place she thought and took a few photographs and then she set about studying the timetables on there and this would be quite easy to understand because she needed to look up numbers for the time and Leeds in letters and they seemed to be quite regular so she shouldn't need to wait for too long.

She wouldn't have needed another ticket but she was not to know that and got herself in a blind panic when she realised the ticket office was closed and it seemed all tickets had to be purchased by way of the machine she was now staring at for which she had no change. She looked outside of the station but she could not have picked a more remove and desolate place as there was not one single person in the vicinity. She paced up and down completely at a loss as to what to do and set about walking to find a passer by or at least some sort of convenience store but all with no joy.

As she walked back towards the station she noticed a white van with a male driver pull onto the tiny car park and ran across to him and in her customary broken English asked the man "Excusing me are you having any change?" The man looked at her in a strange way but smile to gain her confidence as he led her back towards the station. Julie Hartson and Mei Ling had never met, they were both from different continents, from different eras.

Had different tastes in music , their cultures were poles apart but for one day alone they would share something in common. They had both arrived in this world at different periods in time but they would both depart this world on the exact same fateful day, fate had deemed they would both meet their maker within a few hours of each other.

Mei Ling smiled and thanked the man for his assistance and walked alongside himself, cheerfully, little knowing the fate that awaited her!

Chapter Twenty Six

Rick had been driving along quite leisurely and he wasn't particularly in any rush to get anywhere. He was visibly relaxed now and he had put a great deal of distance between himself and the heavy police presence that had engulfed Dewsbury.

He would always feel comfortable whilst walking with the kinder egg inside of him because it always seemed to nestle in the same spot with little discomfort but for some strange reason it would become quite annoying whilst he was driving and so he had taken it out and hidden it in a safe and secure hiding place on the dashboard.

He drove along casually taking in all of the scenic route but at the same time always looking for an easy target to return and burgle at some time should he choose to do so.

He noticed the road sign indicating there was a railway station close by and due to the serenity of the surroundings and how quiet the area appeared to be this could be a likely target.

He pulled up on the tiny car park and was taking in all the surroundings and plotting his escape route when out of the blue he was approached by a complete stranger of Chinese origin and he could barely understand a word she was saying but he got the gist of it , that she was requiring some loose change.

He smiled at her and didn't wish to scare her away by being a loofe, he had already looked around in all directions and it would be quite easy to bundle her into the van and do with her as he wished at a later stage.

He was running lots of different ideas and methods through his head but he also realised that it could represent a problem driving around with a live hostage until he could kill her.

Why take that risk he thought when this seemed a perfect setting. He had glanced around time after time and had never even witnessed anyone else to be around except for the two of them.

He kept staring into her face as she babbled on and on he had no patience with foreigners at the best of times but the chinese just seem to talk too fast for Rick's liking.

He was thankful when an inter city train hurtled through the station at great speed because it drowned out what she was saying and Mei Ling pit fingers in both of her ears to cancel out the noise.

They both laughed once the train had passed but in an instant Rick had an inspirational thought of what he was going to do and it would be a perfect ending to what lay ahead.

He would get his kill with little or no mess and he could drive away having committed a near perfect murder.

He patted his pockets indicating that he understood that she was asking for change and then he put one finger up indicating for her to wait whilst he searched for further loose change in the cab of the van.

He did have few doubts about what he was about to do but they soon died away the very moment he placed his hand around the plastic shell and unscrewed it to retrieve a gold coin.

He was sexually aroused and he knew there would be no going back, they walked together back towards the station and only stopped once whilst Rick studied in detail the train schedules and his main interest would be the arrival of the next inter city train in whichever direction.

He would need to stall her for the best part of five minutes and engaged her in

conversation but for the majority of the time
gave her the impression that he was struggling
to understand her.

As the time of the train crept ever so closer
Rick pulled a lot of coins out of his pocket
and indicated with his finger for her to
follow him.

She had no reason to doubt his intentions
and thought perhaps he was leading her to
another ticket machine as he had pointed at
this one and gave her a gesture that indicated
it was broken.

She crossed the bridge with him to the
platform where she had earlier got off of the
train.

As they paced up and down she gave Rick
a nonplussed look and shrugged her shoulders
when there didn't seem to be another change
machine.

Rick turned her head to face him because
at the moment he wanted to strike he wanted
to be able to look at the fear in her eyes when
she seen the approaching train speeding
towards her.

She thought Rick had reached into his pocket
to once again bring some change out but
instead he reached forward and placed a gold
coin in her pocket and within the same
movement gave her the gentlest of nudges and
although her arm reached out instinctively to
grab a hold of Rick's arm to save herself that
would be impossible because rick had taken

that half a step back to ensure his safety and Mei Ling fell straight into the hurtling path of the train giving her no chance of survival whatsoever.

Her eyes seem to stare through rick with the question … Why?
But Rick would never know the answer to that himself. He lit a cigarette and calmly walked out of the station and drove away never giving any thought to the fact that he had killed yet again.

The village he just drove through had to be among the sleepiest he had ever come across but he was happy he had chosen not to bundle the chinese girl inside as it could have led to complications. A kill was a kill chose what method he had deployed.

The train driver had reported hitting something or someone and he hoped that it hadn't been another suicide victim because he had hit one of them many years previously and he had been given time off and medication from his doctor to assist in overcoming the trauma of the experience.

Rick stopped at one of the many country pubs to have some food and a pint before continuing his journey to Flamborough Head and completed his journey in the late afternoon of that day and then set about the well trodden route that he and Sarita used to take.

He thought back to the happy smile on her face as she would walk barefoot in the sand very carefree with a problem in the world. He had parked up by Bridlington and walked along the beach towards the cliff tops and because of the fond memories he knew this was about to bring he had decided there would be no more killing and he would lay this period to rest by throwing the plastic egg and it's contents into the sea once the tide had come in.

He thought that would be very symbolic a sort of message in a bottle figuratively speaking, he followed the same procedure they had done as a couple and took his shoes and socks off and placed them behind him and sat and dangled his feet over the edge.

He smiled continually as he reflected back to that period and he could have sat here for the rest of the week he thought to himself.

Julie Hartson had arrived at Thornwick Bay a few hours before and felt a warm glow all around herself as if the childhood memories came flooding back of those special moments.

While she walked along the path on the clifftops she noticed a man sat alone in reflective mood and as she got closer realised he was barefoot and deep in thought.

"Evening! Do you mind if I join you?" she requested but before rick could even raise the slightest objection she had sat by him and began to strike up a conversation.

They both quickly gathered they had gone through complicated relationship issues and the strangest thing about any strangers meeting in these circumstances is how quickly they just open up to each other like it was the most normal thing ever.

On reflection Rick had spoken to no one all day apart from the chinese girl and Julie's last conversation would have possibly been the nurse upon leaving the hospital.

Yet here they were two lost souls and telling each other their most closely guarded secrets . Julie settled very easily in Rick's company and soon took her own shoes and socks off and dangled her legs alongside his.

They both expressed their fears for the future and each in turn sympathised with the other ones cause.

He listened intently as she described many of the beating that she had taken and he was at a loss as to understand why a woman would continually put herself through that but she explained it was probably a misguided form of love which eventually needs confronting. She also told Rick that the only other option she had seen available to herself was suicide and on many occasions she had wished herself dead.

Rick seen a few similarities with aritas beatings and her failure to leave but the difference was this was her own father doing the beatings rather than a husband or a lover and his anger levels began to rise to a very high level. Julie seemed to sense this and placed a comforting arm around him but rick was rambling incoherently now and muttering under his breath.

The volcano was close to eruption! They both laid back and strared at the sky and the only interruption was an aged couple walking by with their dog and giggling and tittering about "young love" which angered rick and he sat up immediately very annoyed that the dog walkers were under the impression that he and julie were a couple.

Now for the first time he had began to look closely at her face and decided she was haggard ten years or more older than him and time had definitely not been kind to her. She was beginning to vex him now and especially her favourite topic of conversation which always seemed to revolve around suicide, he excused himself for a moment and pretended he needed to urinate and went behind a bush. He then took his plastic egg from his pocket, took out one coin and replaced the lid.

He returned and sat by julie and was even still prepared to give her a reprieve depending on how the next hour or so passed. Things did not improve very much and the one moment that sealed her fate was when she placed her hand on his inner thigh and stroked it suggesting they could maybe make each other happy even if it was just for a short while. Rick was disgusted!

How dare she even think that she could compare to Sarita, he hid his disgust from her and agreed maybe they could connect in a little while but he prefered talking right now.

The last thing he would want her to do was stand up and walk away because he had offended her because he had now decided that she was going to die.

His words seemed to placate her and they both shared a cigarette and entered into conversation again and then Rick had looked all around to confirm that nobody was about and then prepared himself but he would want the full package not only the murder but the fearful eyes that accompanied it. "I've got something to tell you Julie" he said and then staring directly into her face he informed her that he had killed six people since he had come out of prison.

Her mouth dropped open in shock but then she laughed , albeit, nervously expecting Rick to burst out laughing at any moment and was pulling her leg.

She stared long into his face and once she realise those words were not about to be spoken and rick just sat nodding she became scared and motioned to stand but rick had already placed his hand in the small of her back and guided her over the cliffs and to the depths below.

Again he felt no remorse and she had spoken of death that often that he felt she should embrace it she had not been brave enough to go through with any suicide so Rick felt he had given her that final helping hand she so obviously craved.

He stood up and looked around to confirm the area was clear of any prying eyes, he put his shoes and socks on and walked away after placing a gold coin into the victim's shoes.

Chapter Twenty Seven

God how he wished it could have been Sarita
who had shown up and sat by him on the cliff
top and some sense of normality could have
returned.

He still had every intention of returning to
the spot at regular intervals in the hope of
at least seeing her again.

They had always promised each other they would
meet there again one day but he was feeling
so despondent right now he even felt like
throwing himself off the cliff.

Even the kill hadn't appeased him none and the
last two he had killed had not brought about
much satisfaction.

He drove further along the coast and spent a
few days in Scarborough and there appeared to
be headlines mentioning the two latest deaths
so he took matters into his own hands and set
about sending a chilling memo to James O'Dowd.

He carefully cut letters from a newspaper and
a magazine and with them glued a letter to him

giving a picture portrait of all the events
that had involved the coins and gave a brief
description of victims involved and once he
was satisfied he packaged it up and addressed
it to the officer and placed it inside the
nearest post box and set off on the journey
home.

He reflected on much of Julie's conversation
and thought to himself at least she was at
peace now and in just the same way he felt he
had assisted the alcoholic he believed he had
saved them any more suffering and in some way
condoned his behaviour.

Instead of killing random people he wished he
had the courage to just walk upto Sarita's
brothers or her father even and just kill them
on the spot but what purpose would that serve.
It wasn't like it would help him win her back!
It would have the opposite effect and he would
be looking at a very lengthy prison sentence.

Dewsbury was still on hive of activity and he
would need to be wary of which areas he visited
because racial tensions were at an all time
high with many communities divided. Not many
people could be found on the streets of an
evening and the few that were about had been
advised to walk about in couples.

They had nothing to fear because Rick had once
again placed the egg up his rectum and he had
no intention of killing again, his blood lust
had been satisfied for the time being and he
was looking forward to some of the events that

were about to unfold.

He already seen the worried frowns on O'Dowd's face and he wanted to add to them. He would have loved to be a fly on the wall when the package was opened.

He intended keeping a low profile for a while anyway and he doubted the police had made much headway since he had last been in the area. O'Dowd was already on his second coffee since arriving at the office and he hadn't got round to looking through his in tray yet.

He walked across to the incident board and had a few discussions with his colleagues and then finally after the package had laid there for perhaps three hours he pulled it out from among the pile of letters and memos that were also in the tray.

"Everybody stop what you're doing and get over here now" he demanded.

He spread the contents out very carefully and did not wish to disturb any forensics that may exist.

This could be the killer's mistake, many killers he had met down the years had thought they were superior to any police investigation but one such as this who wished to tease and taunt the police were very rare indeed.

He looked at the indications suggesting there were six murders and he was more than intrigued because he was only aware of the four.

"I want to fucking know immediately who the other two are" and he hoped more bodies weren't waiting to be discovered in Dewsbury because it would give 'the super' a heart attack.

No matter how clever the killer thought he was there would always be those little mistakes that would give detectives a clue here and there.

They had been working with nothing but assumptions before but this letter would be a minefield of information.

He cursed the day the post office invented self adhesive stamps but saving said that he doubted the killer would leave any traces of saliva. Even so he wanted everything checking at the lab.

After making detailed photographic copies of everything that existed he had the original hand delivered in a bag to the forensics laboratory.

He pinned what he had on the incident board and stood back and inspected over and over the most important piece of evidence they had thus far.

He contacted the police forces in the country that the postmark on the envelope covered and wanted to know of any suspicious deaths in the previous and especially what appeared to be a picture of a Chinese lady and he stressed the importance of being aware of any gold coins.

"The bastard had even been on holiday and killed." thought O'Dowd or maybe he even lived at the coast and had visited Dewsbury to kill. He had to keep all options open to himself. Albrighton attempted to address some of the officers who had gathered around but O'Dowd's patience had finally snapped with him and he pointed to a chair and told him to sit in it and not utter another word. He told him he was now assuming command and that if he wished to work alongside him then that was fine but if he didn't he pointed to the door and reminded him that was the way out and also informed him that should he choose to take it upstairs he would telephone the regional commander.
O'Dowd had had enough now and the envelope and its contents had been addressed to him and the taunts were directed at him and if anyone was going to bring this bastard to book then it was going to be him.
Albrighton seemed to sense this was no time to argue because everyone in attendance had given O'Dowd a round of applause at the speech he had just given and it seemed that they had welcomed the fact that he had once again stamped all of his authority over the case. Telephones were ringing on most desks now as little snippets of information came flooding in. Apparently a Chinese woman had been found

but it may be a lost cause as it seemed to be a suicide.

When O'Dowd discovered that the girl was from Leeds he decided to follow up this lead himself and travelled the few miles to Leeds to speak to the next of kin himself. Her uncle explained to him that yes of course she was a little concerned that immigration would remove her from the country but certainly not enough for her to wish to take her own life. He showed him recent family photographs of what appeared to be a very happy girl who constantly smiled and he knew instantly that the girl's death had been misinterpreted and she had in fact been murdered. His gut instinct knew this to be the case but where was the coin?

He sent a colleague to chase up any useful information the train driver may have to shed any further light on the matter but he could neither confirm nor deny that anyone else was stood on the platform with her so that could still suggest it was a suicide but O'Dowd refused to accept that.

He contacted the morgue where the body had been taken and asked them could they send him any details of her possessions at the earliest opportunity. Her uncle had said she was a very keen photographer and took her camera everywhere with her. He wanted to get a hold of that camera because of the possibility she had taken a snapshot of her assailant without him knowing what a long shot that would be. But he persisted because had the bit between his teeth.

From the office being a defected sombre place to work the previous weeks everyone was now running about constantly active with sheets of paper in their hands in a state of frenzied excitement. This was what he enjoyed, this is what police work was about and he was proud to be a part of it notwithstanding that he also held the reins again.

He was the captain of the ship again and he would guide his men through whatever stormy weather that was placed in their way.

So this bastard had chosen to have a battle with him had he? Well let the battle commence and he would savour the moment when placed a pair of handcuffs around your wrists and stood you in front of a crown court judge.

His telephone rang and it snapped him from his thoughts and once he confirmed that he was inspector o'dowd a voice at the other end confirmed that although much of the clothing had been shredded along with the body he had just found a strange foreign gold coin in the pocket of the victim. "BINGO" exclaimed o dowd and thanked the man and said one of his colleagues would soon be on the scene to gather any of the evidence they may need.

He made the sign of the cross and said a small prayer because what an horrific fate she had met for being in the wrong place at the wrong time.

Just an innocent girl so smiling and full of
life who had travelled thousands of miles in
the hope of bettering herself . He swore to
himself he would bring justice to Mei Ling and
all of the other victims.

Who could possibly be so mentally deranged to
think it's the right thing to do to push an
innocent girl under the path of a speeding
train knowing the only outcome would be for
her to be severely mutilated.

This one girl alone and the method of her death
would inspire o'dowd to walk through walls to
capture the culprit. "We have another victim"
he informed everyone as he pinned Mei Ling's
photograph to the board.

DEtective Sergeant Williams came storming in
and proclaimed "We may have another one Gov"
It came as no surprise to o'dowd because the
letter had already indicated this and the news
from williams was that dog walkers had found
shoes and socks which had been handed into the
lost property office on the caravan camp site
and no one had thought anything of it until
a body had washed up on the shore and the
community constable responsible for this
sleepy little area had only that morning read
a fax to all serving policemen to watch for
any unusual circumstances concerning
fatalities.

Once the woman had been formally identified
and the news had filtered through of her many

years of domestic abuse and her recent discharge from hospital it seemed to be yet again a clear cut case of the woman taking her own life.

The constable in question thought it strange that she chose to take her shoes and socks off and upon further investigation discovered the missing items and once he stood the shoes on end a gold coin dropped into the heel section of the shoe.

He was careful not to handle it and smudge any evidence that may be on it.

O'dowd could not praise the man highly enough. This was good honest policing at grassroots level and he congratulated all of his men because in the space of a day they had managed to not only locate the victims but also put a name to them too.

The killer may have thought he had sent them a jigsaw puzzle to complete and occupy them but their mission had been completed in double quick time and how o dowd wished he had a forwarding address to notify the killer of this.

He had the next best thing though as he called a press conference and wished the story to be in that evening's editions and he now addressed the local and national tv stations of the latest slayings.

"Touché" he thought with the killer in mind but this was no personal duel and he would need to remember this and remain very professional.

Chapter Twenty Eight

Sarita had heard on the news of some poor girl
being murdered at the very same spot where her
and Rick had first become passionately
embroiled with each other and with all that
was happening in her home town of Dewsbury she
doubted very much that all of her restrictions
would be lessened anytime soon.

She hoped Rick had managed to keep himself
safe while all of these murders were happening
and she would have given anything to feel his
arms around her one more time.
Her aunt accompanied her everywhere but there
would be that one moment when she took her eyes
off the ball and her chance would come. She

had , had half an opportunity a few days before but had decided against it because her money funds were indoors. If she had had that money with her at the time she had no doubt she would have seized the opportunity .

At that moment of reflection it sent a shudder down her spine to think that she had made her escape and made for the North Coast that could just as easily been her who was murdered on that hilltop.

"God! There were some crazy people in the world" she thought and she was thankful she had met herself a nice man in Rick.

They would meet again one day of that she had no doubt but for now she would keep doing her daily chores and smiling pleasantly at her aunt.

"So he is not as foolish as he first looks" thought Rick as he listened to o dowd addressing the concerned public.

His biggest task now to overcome was the fact that Rick had decided to retire for a little while so how could o'dowd be expected to complete the full jigsaw no other pieces were available to insert?

Rick wasn't likely to make anymore mistakes, he knew it had been a little foolhardy to actually post the letter to o dowd but he couldn't resist being able to bait him.

Meanwhile o'dowd attended both of the last two victims funerals and carefully scanned the

crowd for any unusual mourners but in his
heart he doubted the killer would put in an
appearance. But at least he had been able to
pay his respects so he hadn't exactly had a
wasted journey.

Hour upon hour of CCTV had been studied
covering all points of entry to the coastal
areas but all to no avail but o'dowd felt that
sometime soon they would get a break… Surely!
Because things had ground to a halt and
somewhere out there was a crazed lunatic who
still had four of these coins in his
possession.

He could strike at anytime and nobody could
possibly pinpoint and say that the killer
lived in Dewsbury, on the coast or anywhere
at all.

It would need a mistake on this man's part for
the case to unfold but at the present time he
had took to the ground like a fox.

Rick spent much of his time in and around
Dewsbury town centre and he was a familiar
figure in many of the local public houses.

He had decided the best policy was to be seen
and therefore giving out the impression he was
a normal run of the mill bloke with nothing
to hide. Perfectly normal person who just
liked a few pints.

He mixed with all of the regulars and played
pool and discussing menial topics like the
weather and the football, he was good at
blending in and was recognised as a stand up

guy and nobody had a bad word to say about him. Rick was quite brazen and would green any uniformed officers walking the beat in the time although he would limit the conversation to small talk. He was creating an image for himself and it seemed to be working quite well not one person saw him as a threat.

He got himself a little work as a man with a van and moved items from place to place usually furniture and only as and when he needed to do so so he could choose to work only on the days he would need to.

Meanwhile it had all gone very quiet at the station and some days the simple report of a missing person would cause alarm bells at the station with the concern that he may have struck again and out of his hole.

Rick had took to his everyday routine like a duck to water and he was confident in himself knowing that if he chose not to kill again then the likelihood would be that he would never be apprehended and it would just become another cold case.

He decided to stay well away from the north coast because he was sure that other measures would have been put in place to monitor incoming and outgoing traffic. He was sure traps would have been set and he had no inclination to be caught in one of those snares.

O'dowd would check his mail the very minute he got into work each day but he knew after a period of time that this was unlikely to happen a second time.

The one good thing that had come out of it was Albrighton had been transferred back to his own unit after one or two complaints upstairs about his behaviour from colleagues he could once twist around his finger. The novelty had worn off it seemed and not too many enjoyed working alongside him.

Linda Peterson was the only one who seemed to be a little disturbed by him no longer around and she probably felt quite foolish but o'dowd was a very forgiving man and things soon returned to normal and the unit was one big family again. Normal service had been resumed and now there was just a small matter of bringing a murderer to justice. There would be more chance of doing that now there were no divisions amongst them.

There had been much criticism of the West Yorkshire Police on previous mass murders and O'dowd was determined that his task force would not be facing the same level of abuse. Rick rented himself a room above one of the town centre shops and remained in the lion's den. The police would have been surprised to learn that their killer resided perhaps one hundred yards away from the station and cell they had waited eagerly to place him in.

He had not done this intentionally it just seemed a natural progression that he had found accommodation and a little work and he hadn't set out to live this close to the station it had just happened. He could no longer live in the van because apart from furniture removals he was occasionally disposing of large amounts of work related refuse.

His only lapse and link with his previous lifestyle was he had begun to smoke heroin again and he just couldn't help himself he found it had a calming effect on him and after chasing a little of the "brown sugar" on some tin foil the very last thing he would wish to do was go out and look for other victims.

He wanted to curb that side of his behaviour and lay it to rest. His room was his little retreat after a day's work and he enjoyed the peace and tranquility and if he wanted to smoke a little heroin that was his choice and rather that than unleash the beast.

Saritas aunt, meanwhile in Rochdale , had realised she had forgotten to pay for her parking and asked Sarita to go and put the coins in and place the ticket on the car while she remained in the shop and waited for her to return.

Finally her guilt edged , opportunity had come about and she wasted no time in taking advantage of it. She was kind enough to fulfil her task for her aunt and put the tickets in the windscreen but from thereon she strode in a completely different direction to the shop and although her heart beat increased initially she soon regained her composure and walked towards the local bus station and although she became a little unnerved at the thirty minute wait it soon passed and she clambered aboard mindful to sit away from the window and Rochdale was soon a fading memory as the coach full of holiday makers began its journey to Scarborough. The closest port of call to where she wished to go.

She cared little that she had no change of clothing because she felt in her heart that she would eventually find Rick and he would look after her. She had a reasonable amount of money to last her until that time came but she would not be denied and had a growing confidence about her because this is possibly the bravest thing she had ever done. She felt that in a wave of the she had displaced every barrier that had ever been in front of her. There could only be one logical solution though and that would be to find Rick because she had taken the ultimate leap and she know she could never return to her family.

The journey passed peacefully and she smiled and played with a few of the children, only once did she face any awkward questions as one of the passengers asked why she was travelling alone but she just informed them that she was a returning school teacher in Scarborough which seemed to satisfy the inquisitive lady passenger.

Alighting the bus on arrival she made straight for the camping and hardware shop because she had wanted a sleeping bag for when the night fell in.

She then travelled on another two buses until she could see the cliff tops almost from the upper tier of the bus and she got off very excitedly.

By now she was a little hungry and purchased some food to take with her and have a little picnic on the one spot that she treasured more than any other in the world, she satisfied her appetite and then went and sa on the cliff edge dangling her bare feet over and was mesmerised by the sea and the crashing of the waves. She turned her head away only when she seen anyone approaching half expecting Rick to appear at any given time.

The path of true love never runs smooth was a saying Sarita was familiar with and it certainly appeared the case here. She eventually became tired and got herself in the sleeping bag and soon went to sleep.

It had been a long and tiring day and the excitement had taken it's toll, once she awoke she concealed her sleeping bag amongst the nearby bracken and set off for a long stroll to refresh herself and bring life to her body she would always return to the same spot because she was fearful that Rick may show up one time and she would miss him.

She had no alternative but to do this for however long she needed but the thought had also crossed her mind that she may have to be adventurous enough to venture to Dewsbury to locate him. She could wear a veil and disguise herself if need be.

He already knew he no longer lived at the accommodation that they shared and her only hope of finding the proverbial needle in the haystack was Rick's white van which she recalled fondly.

She felt a little sad knowing someone had died in this very spot where she was sat and closed her eyes and said a few quiet prayers until the voice disturbed her "Excuse me miss, are you aware of recent events on the cliff?" the police relayed to her, he advised her it would not be wise for her to be up here unaccompanied.

The last thing she wanted was to be involved in anything to do with the police as she imagined her frantic parents,by now, would have reported her missing. She was old enough to make up her own mind and it wasn't as if they could force her to go back but she would just prefer there to be no reported sightings of her declaring her to be safe but not wishing to return home.

The policeman had made her mind up for her, she would need to go to Dewsbury. The only alternative would be to sleep on this cliff top each day and night and she now realised the probability of finding him there would be far greater and should she find him quickly enough they could then leave again albeit this time as a couple.

Chapter Twenty Nine

The desk sergeant rang up to O'Dowd's office, and said there was a Mrs Robinson here to see him, and she said it was quite important. O'Dowd had said can you not deal with it yourself, we are dealing with a murder inquiry up here.

"Sorry sir! She is insistent you are the only one she will speak to, and it's very important.

O'Dowd made his way down the stairs and tried to remember that blasted song, Mrs Robinson... and here's to you Mrs Robinson. He hummed it over and over in his head as he descended he stairs, but the name would not come to him.

He entered the reception area to see a little old lady with a newspaper in her hand, and she began to tell him that she had been in hospital for a long time having amendments done to her hip, and he had already decided she was about to talk a lot of meaningless nonsense, so he returned to the pop quiz in his head, and he was pleased with himself that he had remembered Simon and Garfunkel as being the singers.

He had focused on the woman's lips which were rattling like a machine gun about some story of her stay in the hospital, and on her discharge she had been reading through some of the newspapers stacked up at the back of her door, and she had come across an appeal for witnesses to contact James O'Dowd.

She went on to explain that she had seen the man limping away from the taxi, and at the time she thought he was simply dodging paying the fare.

"Ooh, I've never been in a police station before" she said as she looked around and O'Dowd had began to think she was an attention seeker, and was about to turn on his heel, and explain to her he was a very busy man.

"But seriously," she declared "He was always a bad lad was Ricky!".

O'Dowd turned around and said "Which Ricky would that be Mrs Robinson?".

"Ricky Ashcroft" she replied and O'Dowd put a protective arm around her, and led her inside, and Mrs robinson oohed and aahed now as she seen more and more of the interior.

"Someone make Mrs Robinson a drink of tea." he ordered, and as he passed Linda Peterson on the stairs he shouted out for her to run a check on a Richard Ashcroft, and to make it pronto.

This was the break he had been waiting for, until he remembered there was no gold coin with the taxi driver slaying, but even so if they had not found their serial killer it could still prove a significant arrest if they could take another killer of the street.

He treated Mrs Robinson in a very soft mannered approach, and even though old people went all around the house before telling the story he was quite happy to let her do so, because her memory banks had logged every lost detail of that night. She even knew that he drove a white van, and that had been parked outside of an house of Dewsbury Mour and it just got better, and better as she claimed they were a lovely couple called Caron and Mick.

He scribbled the names on a pad and told a colleague "Pay them a visit" and if they aren't very willing, then to bring them down to the station. "Put pressure on them" O'Dowd barked.

Mrs Robinson had more cups of tea in that

hour long statement than he would drink in an whole shift, but he was happy to let her ramble on.

She apologised for not reporting earlier, and went on to explain just what had taken place during the operation, and O'Dowd just smiled sympathetically, and once he thought she had no more to say he asked her how would she like to have a ride home in a police car. She sprang to her feet, and that was even with her bad hip, and almost danced with delight. He knows he would have needed to offer her something a little special because had he not he could imagine her wishing to stay there all through the night talking.

He seemed to have a killer not the killer he wanted, but at least the net was closing in on this one.

Father Hinchliffe's conscience had been troubling him for a long time due to the man's "confession" or seemingly confession and with all of the bad events taking place in the town lately how could he forgive himself if this man was responsible.

He had looked through old school and church christening photographs and he couldn't swear to it but he was almost sure this was Richard Ashcroft. He had looked at the photo time after time. He looked such a quiet, calm little boy but if the father had guessed right that it was him then something was seriously troubling this young man.

He turned off his bedside lamp and promised himself he would contact the police as soon as he woke up the following morning!

Mick and Caron had insisted they wouldn't be saying anything when they were brought down to the station and Mick needed to be restrained with pepper gas he was struggling so hard and it took four officers to manhandle him into the cell.

They both insisted that they wished to remain silent and both demanded legal representation.

O'Dowd decided to show his hand and explain to them the implications of being charged with accessory to murder.

He had told Mick first and then closed his cell door and gave him a little time to reflect on what he had just told him and before very long Mick rang his service button bell and asked would it be possible to confer with his wife.

After due deliberation between the p air they both agreed to make a statement detailing Ricks movements whilst he stayed in their home and O'Dowd thanked them and assured them it was the right thing to do in the circumstances.

They were released without charge and informed they should discuss this with no one or they could find themselves arrested for aiding and abetting an offender.

It totally went against the grain with them to assist the police but even they could not condone murder and they had no regrets.

So now O'Dowd sat with the statement on his desk and tried to build up a picture. They already knew there had been suspicions that the taxi driver was a known heroin dealer and O'Dowd presumed this had been a robbery.

Caron and Mick had confirmed that Rick had a substantial amount of heroin in his room.

What had Mrs Robinson said? That she had seen Ricky "limping" away. O'Dowd dismissed the limp and presumed he did not have a lace in his shoe because that is what he used to strangle the driver. He did not want to let his mind race away with assumptions but the one thing he was sure of is that he had found his murderer and it was now needed to build a watertight case.

He ordered his men to locate Ashcroft and where he was living and what he was driving but do nothing else except place him on a round the clock surveillance. He must not be spooked at any cost because just maybe if he can kill once he can kill again so take it slowly and watch his movements.

O'Dowd slept soundly that night and was pleased to have conducted a good day's police work, and it was the most positive thing to have happened in the department for many months.

The van had been located and put on a twenty four hour watch but as of yet the suspect had not been sighted but they were sure it would only be a matter of time.

O'Dowd had been notified and had requested to be kept posted on even the slightest detail. He got himself a coffee from the machine and sat on his chair with his feet on the table comfortable in the knowledge that at least one arrest was imminent.

His phone rang and he was told that a father Hinchcliffe was at the other end of the line. O'Dowd told them to put him through.

"Good morning father! Please tell me this is some divine intervention". They both laughed and father Hinchcliffe apologized for interrupting him from his duties and said he would feel rather silly if he had misread the situation and it was a false alarm.

He went on to explain to O'Dowd of the evening of admission in the confessional box and said he only felt foolish because the man had proclaimed that he might have killed someone rather than that he had actually done so.

"I understand father" O'Dowd replied "would it be against you religion bounds for me to enquire of a name?" the priest hesitated but he had come this far so he may aswell see it through. "Richard Ashcroft" he said as his words faltered a little.

O'Dowd spat out his coffee and said for the priest to stay where he was and he would be with him in no time.

When O'Dowd arrived at the church the priest appeared to be a troubled soul until he was

assured that he had done the right thing,
because the man had indeed committed a murder.
The priest relaxed on hearing this news, and
it eased his conscience a little.
He was invited down to the station to make a
statement strictly between themselves and he
informed him that no arrest would be getting
made at this time and asked the priest for
complete   discretion   on   what   they   had
discussed for the time being.

     He felt a little foolish even asking this
from the holy man because if you can't expect
a man of god to keep a secret then what hope
is there.

     He asked him would he be prepared to make
himself available to attend an identification
parade if the need aose and he indicated that
he would be willing.

     Sarita had arrived back in Dewsbury and
set about attempting to track Rick down and
she remembered a few of his haunts and friends
and someone informed her that they had seen
him   recently   doing   a   little   furniture
removals and he parked his van a lot in the
car park by the bus station but they couldn't
help her as to where he was living.

     To her great delight she found his van in
next to no time and her heart was racing as
she felt she was getting closer.and closer to
him.

     She certainly couldn't stay here by the
van for any great period for fear of bringing

attention to herself in this hugely populated
muslim area.

She wrote a note and put it behind his
windscreen wiper and asked him to wait at the
van and she would come see him, and went on
to say she had missed him and was deeply in
love with him.

She walked away with the intention of
returning every few hours until they were once
again in each other's arms.

An undercover officer observing notified
O'Dowd of the strange sighting and actions of
this muslim lady and insisted that he wanted
to know what was wrote on the note but
without blowing their cover.

A quick change of clothing was all that
was required and before anyone could even
think anything untoward was taking place a
supposed "traffic warden" ambled from car to
car to apparently inspecting for non payment
of parking and once he realised the coast was
clear he slid the note from the wiper, quickly
photographed it and replaced it in it's
original position and left the site.

"So our killer has a girlfriend does he?
O'Dowd declared and at least they had now more
likely confirmed that he should also be in the
area and not just his van and they had the
added bonus of being able to trace him though
his girlfriend.

Things could not have worked out any better
than if O'Dowd had planned it himself.

Rick had been fortunate for a long time but
as in all lucky streaks they would all come
to an end eventually.
The timing could not have been any worse for
Rick.

Chapter Thirty

Rick had bought cigarettes and a
newspaper and headed for his van with the
intention of having a little lunch at the cafe
and then completing a job he had started the
previous day.

He noticed some woman with a shawl over
her head and face and shouted demanding to
know what she was doing as she appeared to be
trying the passenger door to gain access.

His heart skipped a beat with the
realisation it was Sarita and they threw their
arms around each other and kissed
passionately.

They both has a hundred questions for each

other but he sensed Sarita felt a little unsafe out on the streets and so he suggested they go to his home.

"Don't lose sight of them" O'Dowd demanded, "we need an address for this one"!

They practically skipped along the streets holding each other's hands tightly. It had seemed an eternity since they had last seen each other and they had a lot of lost time to make up.

Rick almost threw the door to his flat off it's hinges in his haste to get in and he threw Sarita on the bed and hastened to join her, but she had seen a few items to cause her alarm and she sat up bolt upright and demanded that he explain about the block and burnt tin foil at the side of his bed on the dressing table.

She got off the bed and was furious that he seemed to have been telling her lies and he was a heroin user.

He attempted to explain to her that he had only had a problem with it since her brothers had been injecting him with it and he had been weaning himself off it slowly but surely by smoking it and he was almost clean and now she was back in his life he could complete the task very much easier.

She was angry and unsure just what to believe and stormed off and locked herself in the bathroom to consider what she should do.

Rick kept talking to her through the door whilst all the time looking around the room for any further evidence of his drug abuse. He opened the window and threw a few pieces of burnt foil out of the window.

He thought he saw two men out in the yard acting suspicious but he thought no more of it because he had the much more pressing matter of Sarita to deal with.

He remembered he had left a small bag of heroin in the bedside drawer and raced across to get it and there sat cosily alongside it was the plastic kinder egg and he quickly unscrewed the cap and placed the bag inside the egg.

He paced up and down and knew full well he could not throw this item out of the window and quickly ha to settle for placing it in ts usual place and up his back passage and he was relieved now believing the room to be clean of drugs.

He had been fortunate but this would be the last bit of luck Rick would be having for a long time.

Sarita finally came out of the bathroom and they sat and discussed the issue. They both agreed that it would be easier to beat the addiction if they left dewsbury were the evil substance was easily obtainable. She could not stay around here anyway for obvious reasons and so Rick began to pack his few belongings together, and vacate the property and area all together to begin a new life together.

It was quite strained between them when they

had reached the van because Sarita was now unsure if she had made the right decision after all, but for now she would need to go with her heart and hope the situation would improve.

They squeezed each other's hand as they drove towards the outskirts of the town and smiled at each other occasionally.

"Don't worry" he assured her "everything is going to be fine"!

By now Rick had noticed a particular red peugeot car on more occasions than he cared to remember, perhaps he was being a little paranoid, but he decided to pretend he was lost and went around the next circular road quite a few times before continuing his journey, but he had not been mistaken as he yet again noticed the car. His Mind raced back to the two men he thought he had seen down in the yard.

He couldn't concentrate and was trying to assess the situation when suddenly a different car pulled out infront of him and he had to break hard and within seconds the windscreen shattered and Sarita screamed in shock thinking it may be her family members. She soon realised different as Rick was dragged through the broken window and thrown face down to the floor with his hands cuffed,and placed behind his back and a gentleman stood over him stating "Richard Ashcroft you are under arrest on suspicion of murder" and then read him his rights.

If Sarita was in shock at this news she was dumbstruck once she was placed in hand cuffs herself and told that she must accompany them to the station.

They were both taken in different cars and kept apart and Rick's mind raced believing he would be receiving many life sentences for the series of murder.

He was booked in and placed in a cell where he paced up and down for long periods until he was informed his solicitor had arrived and he was told they would be interviewing him shortly concerning the murder of a taxi driver outside Dewsbury railway station and reminded him of his rights to remain silent.

Once he was placed back in his cell he was alittle confused. Was they bluffing? Did they know more than they were letting on?

The interview began with various questions regarding the death of the driver,and he became tired of replying "no comment" to each question.

He was very bemused by it all because there had been no mention of anything else connected with other murders. Was they playing a game with him? Would they be introducing further evidence at a later stage?

He requested his solicitor to enquire about the well being of Sarita but was informed that she had been released without charge after making a statement,but they may need to recall

her as a witness at a later date should Rick
choose toenteranot guilty plea.
It seemed there was now no hope what's so ever
of himself and Sarita ever being in what could
be deemed a relationship ever again, and he
couldn't blame her really so he now had to
think of himself as his self preservation
instincts kicked in.
"What the fuck was going off here" he thought
to himself as yet another bout of questioning
continued but only concerned with the death
of the taxi driver.
He still denied being involved each time he
was quizzed,but they now informed him that
they would be putting him on an identification
in front of two witnesses, and that they
already had written statements from friends
of his detailing his heroin use whilst he
lived with them.
Upon returning to his cell once again assessed
the situation and although he felt a little
betrayed by Mick and Caron he also appreciated
the pressure they may have been under.
Who would be the other two witnesses though?
Why were they still only focusing on one
murder?
He eventually stood alongside five other
males who had been chosen from the street, and
was told he could change places at any time
he requested.
The first witness ambed in and after slowly
walking down the first line Rick thought "who

the hell is this crazy old bat"?

She stopped in front of him and simply said "what have you been upto now Ricky"? And in a flash he remembered her from his younger days s being interfering busy body. She left the room but Rick was still unsure to what she had actually witnessed?

He was very curious as to who the next witness could possibly be but his mouth dropped open when he seen Father Hinchcliffe make his way down the line and stopped at Rick and touched him on the shoulder.

Rick screamed obscenities at him and the officer in attendance pulled the priest away for his own safety.

Rick was placed back in his cell and informed that they would be interviewing him again shortly.

They had certainly give him food for thought and he would really need to consider his position and be a little more forthcoming on the next occasion especially when they fed him a little more of the evidence they had against him.

Fortunately Sarita was only deemed to be a girlfriend and she hadn't been questioned to vigorously and so the police were unaware of any excursions and she had conveniently forgotten to mention her brothers holding Rick Hostage so they would not be arrested.

She had sobbed uncontrollably at the station and it soon became obvious she was unaware of any murder and was not even dating Rick at the time of the incident.

Taking into account how high racial tension was running at the moment the last thing the police wanted to do was antagonise the muslim community any further so they released her at the earliest opportunity and suggested that she return to her parents.

Rick was coming to terms with his situation and began to dip his toes in the water to gauge exactly where he stood and what he was facing.

There still hadn't been any mention of the other killings so after a little deliberation with his solicitor he got him to inform the police that he wished to make an admission.

O'Dowd sat across from Rick as he went into great detail about how he had arranged to meet the taxi driver at a secluded spot to purchase heroin and he also admitted that he had gone with the intention of robbing him of his money and drugs but stressed he had no intentions of killing him and it had been a situation that just got out of control.

He had only meant to black him out a little so that he could go through his pockets and he left the scene believing the taxi driver would come around after a short period.

Rick gave the impression that he was very anguished and apologetic about the outcome of that night and put on a very impressive display which the police seemed to believe, Rick appeared full of remorse and had played his hand superbly.

The police were happy to accept his version of events.

O'Dowd even thanked him for being as forthright as he had been.
He locked Rick back in his cell and walked away, actually sympathising with Rick's addiction and the trouble he had now found himself in due to that craving.

He was remanded into custody to await his court appearance and due to him pleading guilty it could be fast tracked through the system once all of the last formalities had been completed.

A deal had already been done with the crown prosecution service and Rick had been charged with the lesser crime of manslaughter.

He was willing to accept that all day long because from believing he was about to spend the rest of his life in prison. He was now stood in the dock at Leeds crown court doing his summing up and going on and on about the evils of the drug heroin and Rick would be totally oblivious to the sermon.

He only wanted the judge to reach the end of the lecture and the only thing he was interested in hearing was the actual sentence which was finally given.

He was to serve six years for manslaughter.

Chapter thirty one

Some of the other prisoners thought Rick to be a bit of an odd ball because he was constantly smiling and laughing to himself around the prison and on the exercise yard and they found that sort of behaviour very strange from a man who had just been given six year term of imprisonment.

He had waited and waited for the dreaded police visit to come with further questions but it had never come and he was now confident that he had escaped justice on them matters, and he had every right to feel happy with himself.

The situation could and should have been very much worse but if he kept his head down and done as he was told he could have been out of there in less than three years.

He would still have his depression days when he reflected back on his time with Sarita but he would need to accept that part of his life was now banished to history.

One day out on the exercise yard as he walked along, everyone preferring to avoid him for his unusual behaviour, he suddenly realised he had company alongside him in the shape of his previous cellmate John Davison who struck up a conversation like he had never been away from Rick, and went on to tell him, all excitedly, that he had been given parole and was about to be released in the coming months.

"How dare he engage him in conversation" Rick thought. He despired the man and if he was honest with himself this was the man who had influenced him to actually go on the killing spree that he just had.

Davison suggested that they ask one of the officers about the possibility of sharing a cell again being as how they had got on so well previously.

"Jesus" Rick laughed at the twisted logic of the man for believing in his sad mind that Rick was his friend.

He stared at the man in disbelief but suddenly Rick had dreamed up a fitting finale for this wife murdering reprobate and he agreed that it would be good if they could share a cell together again.

He would not wish to carry out his plan to soon because it could possibly seem a little strange sohe would wait and choose him moment carefully.

They were both moved in together and Rick opted for the upper bunk and imagined the scenario night after night while he was lay awake.

The conversation has barely changed much from the last time he had been sharing a cell with him. The same old ramblings and him becoming excited when his wife had been in her final death throes.

"Oh i understand that now"! Rick would state but Davison would reply that he could not possibly fully understand to Rick about that final moment.

Rick would luh at him and his ignorance of Rick's misdemeanours during the period of time he had recently been out in the public domain.

He would soon discover on one of the coming nights just exactly how much Rick fully understands Davisons ramblings.

When he had been out of his cell and Rick had been left alone he had set plans in motion to carry out exactly what he had planned night after night for the previous week.

He tore a few thin strips from the cover sheet of his bed and formed them into the shape of a hanging rope that would hold Davisons weight.

He would need to make one for himself also because he hadnow prepared a note confessing to everything about him. He then intended to place a coin i his hands and make him his final victim before he hung himself to bring everything to a conclusion.

He had decided he could wait no longer and that night was going to be the final curtain call for both of them.

Davison watched Rick squatting in the corner puzzled as to what he was doing until he seen the plastic kinder egg in Rick's hand and jumped off the bed.

"What we got buddy" he demanded to know and Rick showed him the bag of heroin he had saved for a special occasion and he couldn't really have found a more ideal situation than the one now.

Rick knew he would need a great deal of courage to take his own life and thought the heroin would make the act a little easier.

He caressed the coins. It was the first time he had even touched them since he had come back in the jail. He had needed to take the egg out daily to complete his toilet duties but would always replace it straight away preferring not to remind himself of that manic period.

Davison was excited at the prospect of smoking some half decent heroin from the street rather than diluted dusty powder that circulated amongst all of the prison population.

He inhaled the smoke frantically and let his head roll back while he savoured the moment and Rick encouraged him to smoke more.

He asked Davison to tell him again about the fateful moments of his wife's death and he began to ramble on and Rick knew word for word the story that would come from his lips.

He had heard it hundreds of times before! But this time Rick waited while he reached the end of his story and once the mention of the sacred bulging eyes entered the story Rick suddenly looped the noose tightly around Davisons throat.

"Like this you mean" he screamed at him as Davisons legs thrashed about to attempt to save himself but he was no match for Rick's strength and the element of surprise had made sure Rick would not encounter much resistance.

He stared into the man's eyes as he choked his last breath out of him.

"Not very nice is it Mister Davison" he laughed into his face as he body went limp.

He threw the body onto his shoulder and after jumping up onto the chair he set about securing the overhang from the noose and around the bars.

He jumped down from the chair and pulled away satisfied the noose was holding the weight and admired his work from the opposite end of the cell.

He sat down and smoked a little heroin himself

to encourage him to find the bravery to carry
out the procedure to himself but he had began
to change his mind believing it to look like
a very unpleasant way to go.
He took the coin back out of Davisons hand and
put everything back in the egg and placed it
back inside himself.
He was careful not to make any mistakes and
he swapped sheets from the beds and put the
torn one on the bed below and he would have
the intact one on the top bunk.
One final look around and then he just
prepared himself to press the panic button and
scream and shout and bang on the cell door.
When they had looked through the spy holeand
seen the body hanging they opened the door
immediately and told Rick to go and wait
outside.
When questioned later he stated that he had
woke up needing to urinate and was deeply
shocked and saddened to find Davison hanging
there.
He went on to add that most nights he would
discuss with Rick how guilty he felt at what
he had done to his wife and he doubted he would
be able to come to terms with everything and
be able to survive once he was released.
He knew he was very depressed but he never got
any indication that he was capable of suicide
or he would have reported him to a member of
staff.
Rick was now placed on the medical win for

observational purposes because apparently it was standard procedure in cases of a cellmate finding the other cellmate dead because of the effects it may have on him.

Rick went along with it but all the time thinking Davison was a piece of trash and good riddance.

He intended to play the game for a short period of time and then return into regular prison population but it had been brought to his attention that prisoners in similar situations previously had been able to apply to the home office regarding an early release on compassionate grounds because of what they had witnessed and the trauma it may have caused.

He lay in his bed on the hospital ward that night and caressed the coins in his hand he had taken from the egg and he became hard.

Maybe the tide had turned and his run of good luck was about to re-emerge. He would leave it for a few months and apply to the home office for them to consider his appeal for an early release.

Every cloud has a silver lining.

May i thank you sincerely Mr Davison for giving me this opportunity.

Rick slept soundly safe in the knowledge he would soon be released and back in the community.

He only hoped he could manage to tame the beast that still existed within him.

79801052R00148

Made in the USA
Columbia, SC
08 November 2017